WALL STREET JOURNAL & USA TODAY BESTSELLING AUTHOR

Sapphire Knight

Sapphire Knight
Copyright © 2020 Bash by Sapphire Knight

Cover Design by CT Cover Creations

Editing by Mitzi Carroll

Proofreading by Marisa Nichols

This book is a work of fiction. The names, characters, places, and incidents are products of the writer's imagination or have been used fictitiously and are not to be construed as real. Any resemblance to persons, living or dead, actual events, locales or organizations is entirely coincidental.

All rights reserved. With the exception of quotes used in reviews, this book may not be reproduced or used in whole or in part by any means existing without written permission from the author.

The author acknowledges the trademarked status and trademark owners of various products referenced in this work of fiction, which have been used without permission. The publication/use of these trademarks is not authorized, associated with, or sponsored by the trademark owners.

WARNING

This novel includes graphic language and adult situations. It may be offensive to some readers and includes situations that may be hotspots for certain individuals. This book is intended for ages 18 and older due to some steamy spots. This work is fictional. The story is meant to entertain the reader and may not always be completely accurate. Any reproduction of these works without Author Sapphire Knight's written consent is pirating and will be punished to the fullest extent of the law.

- This book is fiction.
- The guys are over-the-top alphas.
- My men and women are nuts.
- This is not real.
- Don't steal my shit.
- Read for enjoyment.
- This is not your momma's cookbook.
- Easily offended people should not read this.
- Don't be a dick.
- Romance shaming is slut shaming, don't be that asshole.

DO NOT SHARE

Dedication

To all the women out there who are strong enough to be their own hero. Or, maybe you were forced into being your own hero. Either way, you're a survivor, your own force to be reckoned with. Whether you do that with a man by your side or not, what matters is you, your strength, and perseverance. Here's to you and me, and to *Girl Power* that doesn't have to be thrown in our faces to know we're badasses.

Sapphire Knight

Bash

Kings of Carnage MC

Chaos – President

Hilary Storm

Bash – Vice President

Sapphire Knight

Jinx – Road Captain

Chelsea Camaron

North – Enforcer

M.N. Forgy

Sly – Treasurer

Nicole James

Bouncer

Kim Jones

Special mention of:

Spin - Oath Keepers MC

(Sapphire Knight MC Series)

Common Terms

MC - Motorcycle Club

Ol' Lady – Female significant other

Chapel - Where Church is held

Clubhouse/ Compound – MC home base

Church - MC 'meeting'

Bet – Yes, yep, yeah, okay, fuck yeah, hell yeah, that's what's up…etc.

(You get the picture)

Prologue

If you have everything under control, you're not moving fast enough.

- Mario Andretti

Bash

"I'm out of here." I give a salute to my Kings of Carnage brothers and make my way to the side door. I can handle a beer or two then ride, but I'm not some young asshole anymore who'll ride sloshed out of my mind. Had a buddy of mine die over that shit, and it changed me. I rarely snort the powder I offer up to the sexy dancers either. I did back in the day, but I've grown out of it. Now, it's just a perk I give the girls when they offer me a dance or a bit of information.

My brothers send me off with a nod and promises to see me tomorrow. There's no end to club life; my brothers are my family, and we see each other all the time. It's the way we like things, and the closer we are, the more we trust one another. In our line of work, especially mine, trust is imperative.

It's dark tonight—one of those eerie nights where the clouds hide away the stars and the air's damp. It's humid and a bit sticky, but the breeze is cool. These types of evenings often make for the most comfortable rides. There's not much that holds a candle to riding this late in the South; it reminds me of cruising along the coast in spring. Climbing on my bike, the best sort of feeling washes over me, a peaceful one that I relish.

My bike rumbles with a sexy growl as I crank her over, and the vibrations melt through my skin, fueling my addiction. I'm not some "enthusiast." Riding—as well as my club—has become my life. It's an infatuation running in my blood that I'll never be able to shake, nor do I want to. The fumes from the exhaust hit me, and I slowly release my grip on the brake, coasting out of the bar's parking lot.

Lynyrd Skynyrd croons the "Ballad of Curtis Loew" as I cruise along, struggling to see. My headlight is shit on a black night like this. It flickers, and I begin to curse it as always. The fucking thing never works right, no matter how much I tinker with it.

Just get me home, damn it, I silently chant and pick up my speed. If my light's gonna give me issues, I better hurry the fuck up. I'm not trying to be out here, unable to see shit, attempting to repair the stupid thing. My brothers keep giving me hell for it, yet those fuckers haven't been able to get it to work correctly either.

There isn't a star in sight tonight. The clouds are thick, consuming any light I may obtain from above. I wouldn't be surprised if a dense fog decided to roll in as well. That'd be my damn luck. Singing to myself, I blaze a trail, basking in the wind hitting my skin. The club was busy tonight, and the girls looked damn good. Not a bad way to spend my evening—tits and a cold beer will please any man if they've got their priorities right.

My light flickers off, and I immediately spit out a curse, sitting forward enough so I can bang on the glass. It flashes back on, and I give the loud beast some more gas. I'm hauling ass home before I'm stranded in the middle of nowhere, fuck the dumb shit. I hold on and pay better attention to my surroundings. I don't need any critters running out in front of me.

My phone rings, echoing through my helmet, but I ignore it. Too many distractions and it can wait. My light flashes, turning off again, and I explode, past the point of being patient with the fucking thing. I lean forward, slamming my hand on it, screaming profanities into the eerie cool night. If only I'd had my head up. If only I'd had some way of seeing in front of me...

The crash happens so fast, it's surreal. I feel the initial impact, and then I'm airborne. My radio plays, along with a sickening screech of metal on metal. A horrendous scraping from the asphalt ripping against my baby floods through my mind, then I'm hitting the ground where everything goes black.

Sapphire Knight

Bash

Chapter 1

I don't ride a bike to add days to my life. I ride a bike to add life to my days.

- Unknown

Savannah

I can't believe what I just witnessed. I'm shaken to my core over it. I'd heard the rumble from the motorcycle a ways out. I'd been waiting for it to get close enough so I could maybe flag the rider down. I was hoping they'd possibly have a cell phone I could borrow, and if not, at least have them get a message to someone for me. My phone got shut off last week. I just couldn't afford that luxury right now. Eating is far more important than having a way to communicate with my best friend. The less I contact her, at this point, the better, anyhow.

It's been so quiet out here; it's had me kind of spooked. I'd waited patiently behind my car for someone to drive by, not wanting to sit inside and accidentally doze off. My vehicle's sitting in the middle of the lane, so there was no way someone would miss it. I mean, they'd have to hit me or swerve into the other lane to avoid the beat-up old clunker. I feel so foolish for thinking it was okay to leave it there. Needing help or not,

I just caused this horrific accident by not putting the vehicle in neutral and pushing it to the side.

I can't say I'm surprised I got stuck either; my car had been giving me more and more issues lately. It wasn't anything expensive, but it ran decent when I paid for it with the little bit of cash I had. I'd hit a bump tonight, and it'd died almost immediately. I don't know what on earth would cause it to break. I'm no mechanic. Whatever happened to it killed it completely, though. There isn't power going to anything. I'm stranded in the middle of nowhere, and I don't even have a freaking light or headlights. I feel so stupid for not keeping a flashlight in my car. You live and learn, I suppose. I know one thing, when I get out of this mess, I'll be paying a visit to the dollar store for that emergency flashlight.

As the rider had come close enough to finally see my vehicle, I'd watched his own headlight flicker off, casting us into complete darkness once more. It was too late, however, and his motorcycle and music were far too loud to hear my screams, pleading that he watch out—that he stop.

In what felt like was merely an instant, he'd slammed into my car...the noise was something I'll never be able to free from my mind. It sounded like death, and in the middle of it was him weightlessly propelling through the air. He'd landed off the road into the grassy area, and I ran toward him, screaming, panicking that he was dead...all because of me.

I could make out the shape of his twisted body as I went to him. He lay motionless, and it only fed into my trepidation. *He could be dead, and it's all my fault.*

Everyone knows when your car breaks down, you're supposed to put it in neutral and push it out of the way. Foolishly, I thought by leaving it on the road, it would garner the help I needed, not cause an accident. Everyone knows that's what you do when a car breaks down. I was dumb enough to believe it'd get me the help I need, not cause an accident.

"Oh, God! Please don't be dead!" I cry, already tearing up as I fall to my knees beside his lifeless form. My hands immediately move to touch him, but I pull back at the last second.

What is wrong with me? He could be seriously injured; I probably shouldn't move him.

"Please, this can't be happening." My eyes shoot up to the dark sky, pleading. I don't know if anyone up there is watching right now, but I have to ask. "God, if you're listening, I need your help. This poor man is hurt, and it's all my fault. I'll do anything to make this right...anything!" The tears fall down my cheeks as I begin to sob for this unknown man. "I promise!" I wail. *"Anything!"*

The still man begins to wheeze, moments after my shout of sorrow. I quickly move, shuffling closer, attempting to get a better look at him and his injuries. The murky clouds are beginning to thin out and clear up, the moon and stars peeking through to mock the night. They offer a touch of light to this dimness, and I can eventually make out the man's features a bit better. They're covered in blood and dirt, of course, and my heart aches for him. Crying won't help either of us, but I can't seem to stop. My body shakes with adrenaline, my mind beckoning me to help him, but I'm clueless as to what to do.

This is all my fault.

He wheezes again, and I move to lay his head in my lap. I brush my hand over his scruffy whiskers painted with blood and dust and expel a sigh. He's utterly *beautiful*, no matter he's covered in grime. I can't help but take notice, even a fool wouldn't be blind to his magnificence. I can only imagine how handsome he must be without the tells of the wreck covering his features, how charming his smile is sure to be.

"I'm sorry—so, so sorry," I whisper, repeating myself as a few of my tears fall to his face. I remain over him, cradling his head carefully, hoping to offer him some sense of comfort. My fingers softly pet his scruff, unable to stop from touching him. "Come back. Oh, God, what have I done?" I beg. "I wish I could help you." My eyes clench closed, consumed with grief from accidentally hurting someone this badly. "I don't know what to do to bring you back."

"Shh," comes from my lap with a deep rasp. A large calloused hand reaches up, tenderly cupping my cheek.

Parting my lids, my somber gaze finds the man awake in my lap. I made him wreck, yet he attempts to console me. "Y-you're back? You didn't die?"

His lips tilt into a smirk. "I could believe this is Heaven, and you're an angel, but I don't think my body would be this sore if it were the case."

Biting my lip, I watch him as he continues to stroke his thumb across my cheek. He's catching my tears, staring at me as if I'm the only person he's ever seen. "You wrecked. M-my car is in the road, and you smacked into it. You flew through the air and hit the ground pretty hard. It sounded *so* bad." More tears spill over with my admission, and he reaches for the hand I have against his chest.

He lays his warm, rough palm over it, growing serious. "My headlight went out…I never saw you. Are you all right, darlin'?"

"Me? You're worried about me? I just saw you f-fly through the air. I watched your body hit the ground, and it was terrifying. I thought you were dead."

His brows bunch, his lips pouting a bit before he says, "Of course, I am. Only a dick wouldn't care if you were injured. Now, tell me, did I hurt you when I hit your vehicle?"

I shake my head, my hand lightly moving over his chin. I can't stop touching him, nor do I want to. I'm so thankful he's alive. "I'm okay. You're the one who I thought was going to die. God, I'm *so* sorry."

"I heard you before, Angel. You don't have to keep apologizing to me."

"You could hear me? But you were unconscious. At one point, I wasn't sure you were even breathing. I think you stopped, then somehow started once I prayed."

He shrugs and winces with the move. "I could hear your voice, not anything else. Just you. Sounds to me like you're the one who saved me."

I bite my lip, not sure how to take his words. "Uh, can you move your body?"

"I think so. Did you happen to call the police or anyone else about this?"

Swallowing roughly, I shamefully admit, "I don't have a phone. I wish I could've to get you help. You need someone here to check your injuries."

He relaxes, and with a gesture, he points toward his foot. "Mine's in my boot. Would ya hand it to me so we can take a look at the damage? No need to rush into calling the paramedics when I'm still kicking."

"Yes, of course." I carefully move so as not to hurt him any further. Leaning over his body a bit, I pull up his faded jean leg on the opposite side. I reach into his chunky black leather riding boot and pull out an S9. I hand it over, surprised to see it's still there after what he just endured, and it's not even cracked. I bet he looked sexy dressed in his distressed jeans, boots, white T-shirt and leather vest before all of this happened and covered him in blood and road grime.

He presses the side button, expelling a relieved breath when it illuminates. "Good, it still works."

I bob my head, not sure what else to do as I kneel beside him and watch him. He turns on the flashlight and sits up. At his cringe of pain, I lunge forward to help him. "Be careful!"

He flashes me an amused grin, his sparkling gaze meeting mine again. "I'm okay, sweet pea. Thanks for your concern."

"Please, let me help you." I stand and offer him my hand. If I were stronger, I'd bend down to help lift him, but this is the most I can offer right now. He's got to be wobbly after going through that whole ordeal.

He chuckles and clenches at his ribs with the move. "Fuck!" He hisses the curse. "I think I broke a rib or two in that tumble. They're the worst to crack, they screw with everything."

"You don't seem too upset about it, at least not as much as I would think. Has this happened before or something?"

"Not exactly. I've wrecked before, back when I was a kid. I prefer to stay on my bike; I learned that the hard way."

"Maybe you shouldn't move. I don't want to make it any worse. We should get an ambulance here with a stretcher, especially if your ribs are injured."

He flashes me his beguiled grin again and argues, "I'll be all right, sugar. I'm a man."

I roll my eyes but step away. I'm still close enough to help if he needs it, but I give him a little space to move. If anything, I'm happy to know he's well enough to act a bit macho around me. He finally gets to his feet, hand firmly holding his injured side. He's tall, much taller than he'd appeared to be on the ground. I don't know why, but that detail excites me even more.

"Be careful," I chastise. My concern leaks through, although the only thing I should be trying to do is get out of here as quickly as possible. It's nighttime, and I'm with a bleeding stranger. "Let me hold the light so you can see where you step." I don't think he's used to having a woman help him, but I can't seem to stop myself.

"This is sweet, havin' you fuss over me like this." He completely ignores my cautionary suggestion and takes a hefty step, only to trip and fall down. "Fuck!" The gorgeous brute curses and I move to pick up his phone that's flown a few feet away. "Shit, that hurt," he grumbles.

"I've read that after an accident you can be disoriented and need assistance walking. That's why I offered."

"Well, that makes me an idiot, I suppose," he complains, moving slower to stand this time.

"That's not what I meant, I just…well, never mind. Are you okay?"

He expels a heavy breath and nods. "You…ah…wanna help me out, then? I'll check out your car too."

"Um, sure. Um, you don't have to do that. I mean, really, I made you wreck. This is all my fault."

"Sweet pea—"

"Savannah."

"Huh?"

"My name…it's Savannah. Savannah Mae Lexington."

"Nice to meet ya, Miss Lexington."

"Please, Savannah is fine."

He nods, and I duck under his arm to offer him some added balance. I point his phone in front of us and carefully guide him to take slow steps, so he doesn't fall again. "Pretty name for a pretty girl," he mentions.

"Are you flirting with me right now?"

He chuckles, only to groan in pain. "Just callin' it like I see it. I meant no offense, just stating facts. Kind of hard not to notice your beauty when I have you next to me."

"I'm not offended in the slightest. Just surprised that you're well enough to flirt after a serious accident. It's actually comforting to know you're not completely disoriented."

His grin remains firmly in place, and I find myself drawn to the handsome biker's easy smile. "Do me a favor and pop open your hood, would ya?" he asks as he leans against the front of my car.

"I can't believe you're trying to help me after what just happened," I mumble and climb behind the wheel. I reach down by my leg to pull the hood release latch. It makes a popping sound, and I stare out ahead to watch him mess with the hood latch, moaning and groaning to himself.

"Stay there, Savannah, and crank the engine when I tell you to."

"Yeah, okay."

He lifts the hood with a pained grunt, and I nearly hop out to help. He's a manly man, though, and I'm sure he'd take offense to it, rather than allow me to step in. I still feel a sense of guilt as my car nearly killed the guy, and here he is hurting while attempting to fix it.

There's a bit of clanging around, and the light from his phone is moving all over the space. It illuminates underneath the hood, and it takes everything in me to stay rooted in place as he instructed. I want to see whatever he sees. Maybe I would be able to fix the car myself the next time it breaks down and leaves me stranded on the side of the road.

"All right," he calls out loudly. "Try it now."

Pressing the brake and key in, I turn the ignition switch, and the engine starts right up. My headlights illuminate as well as the interior light, and my radio blares some country song. I hurry to turn the music down and watch as the biker steps away and slams the hood closed. "Oh, my God, thank you!" I cheer, a smile finally gracing my face after all the stress of the evening.

"You're welcome, but, um, could I possibly ask you for a ride? My brothers aren't in the best shape tonight to tow my bike or pick me up. I was coming from the bar." He shrugs, wincing with the move. "I'll have to come back for my motorcycle tomorrow. Hopefully, it's not as bad in the daylight."

The smile drops, and I sniffle, ready to explode with more tears. Knowing his motorcycle is trashed, and he'll be wanting to be compensated for it has sent me into a panic. I couldn't pay him no matter how hard I tried. "I-I have insurance," I stammer, my mind going a million miles a minute, it seems. "They'll pay for it…even if we don't call the cops, right?" The last thing I need is the police over here. I can already imagine the tickets they'll write for my car being in the street and causing an accident. Just one more thing to add to my already dwindling stash of cash. I'm supposed to be saving money, not creating new ways to have to spend it.

He shoots me a puzzled look before shaking his head. "You ever been in a wreck before?"

"No," I admit softly, and gesture for him to get in on the opposite side. He may be a stranger, but after everything we've experienced tonight, I'm not leaving him on the side of the road.

He pulls the door open, and I watch his stiff movements. He easily fills the passenger seat. Although he's not a huge man, he's tall and packed with lean muscle. My little hatchback may as well be a clown car compared to him. The leather vest with various patches makes him look every bit the rebel I'm sure he is. Add in disarray from the wreck, and he appears more like a handsome serial killer or something along those lines.

"I'm sorry, the tiny space must be uncomfortable for you. You can have my jacket to put behind you if you need something to lean against for your ribs. The lever is under the seat if you want to try and get it to move back some more as well."

"Don't worry about it. I'll be fine. Also, just so you know, without us reporting the wreck, the insurance most likely won't pay. Who's your company anyhow?"

More tears fall as I realize that's another indulgence I don't have on this car. Rather than admit it, I say, "I-I didn't pay my bill. I'm so screwed. I'll figure out a way to pay you, I promise." I'm an emotional mess. This wreck has me more sensitive than usual. I thought the man was dead, for Christ's sake; fortunately, he's alive and well enough to hold a conversation with me. "My word is good. I'll prove it to you somehow."

He reaches over and tenderly squeezes my shoulder. "It's okay, Savannah Mae. We haven't seen what my bike looks like. It may not be that serious. I'll take a look tomorrow when it's light out."

I nod, already aware it's a completely mangled mess, and he's far too calm and friendly with me about it. Anything that sounds as bad as it did scraping against the asphalt couldn't possibly be salvageable. "Okay," I agree, even though it's not anywhere close to being all right. I'll pretend for the moment and worry about it tomorrow when he finally grasps the damage. There's nothing I can do about it at the moment, except maybe offer him my tips for the night, and I'm too embarrassed to bring that up right now. I need to catch my breath and come up with a plan. This winging it crap has been completely draining me. At some point, everything has to stop and become normal again.

"One of the cables on your battery came off. That's why your car wasn't working for you. I put it back in place, but it'll need to be tightened, so it doesn't keep happening. If you swing by tomorrow, I can fix it, so it doesn't leave you stranded again."

His words tear me from my self-pitying thoughts. "Oh, you don't have to do that."

"Savannah, if I don't, then someone else needs to. It'll pop right back off at the first decent-sized bump you hit, and who knows when that'll be or where. Just get it tightened, or let me do it. At least you won't have to worry about it anymore."

"Thank you. I appreciate it, really. Where am I taking you, exactly?"

"I was headed home, but you can drop me by my clubhouse instead, as it's closer. It's on this road a ways down, at the old fire station. You'll see the turnoff up ahead on the right with the big garage and whatnot."

I bite the inside of my cheek, keeping my eyes peeled for it. "Okay." Moments later, as the silence becomes too much for me to bear, I find myself whispering again. "I'm *so* sorry for everything."

"Shit happens, and you obviously needed my help. Sounds to me like there was a reason for me wrecking. No telling what could've happened to you out there alone. Someone with shitty intentions could've found you. I'm a bit rough around the edges, but I would never hurt you or anything. Guess it was fate's twisted way of bringing us together." He points and mutters, "Turn right up here…see the reflector?"

I follow his instructions, veering off, and then follow along until a decent sized building comes into view. There are a few bikes and various trucks parked in front.

"This is your club? A motorcycle club?"

"Yep. You can stop by any time, and I'll check that battery for you. You find anything else, you let me know, and I'll see what I can do for you."

"I-I don't even know your name," I admit softly as he opens his door, and the car light illuminates him. He's still covered in blood and dirt, scratched up with a few tears in his shirt. Yet, he's offering to help me out. I'm surprised he hasn't attempted to kill me for ruining his motorcycle and injuring him. I doubt any of the guys I wait on at the restaurant would be this nice to me about making them wreck into my car.

Bash

He offers a sexy smirk and confidently offers, "I'm Bash. The Kings of Carnage Vice President, angel." He winks, and the car door closes swiftly after. I'm left wondering if I'll ever see the bloody, grinning biker again.

Sapphire Knight

Chapter 2

I'm not totally useless, I can be used as a bad example.

- Unknown

Bash

"It's fucked…" I mutter to Jinx, my gut clenching at discovering something I love being ruined. He came along to help me with my bike, and I probably should've come alone. It's the first time I'm seeing it in the daylight, and even I know deep down there's nothing I can do to ride it home today. "Fucking fuck, fuck."

He shakes his head, expelling a breath. "Don't know what to tell you…should've gotten the light fixed."

I shoot him a glower in response. We all checked out that fucking headlight. None of us could figure out what was really wrong with it or fix the damn thing for good. It's embarrassing, to say the least. We ride bikes twenty-four-seven, and a headlight took me out. My brothers will never let me live this down.

"What are you going to do?" he questions as I send a text to North and the prez, giving them a heads up that it's far too jacked up to ride. They were just relieved to know I survived the accident without getting too busted up. I could've died, and Prez would've had my head even after the outcome for leaving him to deal with all the old fucked-up club shit. We've been friends for a long time, compliments of a game of pool and a few bets. The moody bastard counts on me to have his six, and I wouldn't have it any other way.

"Guess the only thing there is to do, is have it towed. Otherwise, it'll take all of us to get it on a damn trailer. I have a bit of cash saved. I'll have to look into finding another bike for the time being. This one won't get me two fucking feet." I shrug, kicking a rock in the direction of the mangled metal. My neck's on fire with the stress of it. I've ridden this bike for five years, even got it airbrushed all fancy and shit. Had it done by an Oath Keeper called Spin when we rode through Texas a while back. "It'll be a bit before I have something this nice again, that I don't doubt."

"It's a shame," he replies.

I grumble, more to myself, chastising, "Fuckin' headlight! What are the odds I'd run into a broken-down car in the middle of the goddamn road?" My fists clench, the sensation of wanting to lay into something hitting me fiercely. The brothers call me Bash because I have a habit of bashing objects with my fists. I'm not some roided-up psycho or anything, just like to hit things when I'm pissed.

I find my buddy's number who owns a local tow service and shoot him a text. I include the location and the service I need, so he has a heads-up to bring along help. He replies instantly, and I meet Jinx's gaze. "He'll be here in twenty. I appreciate you coming with me."

He nods, and we leave it at that. This is just a small piece of our brotherhood. We always have someone around when we need 'em. Having each other's backs is non-negotiable, and I wouldn't have it any other way.

Sapphire Knight

"Hey, VP, a chick's out front asking for you," North grunts, his voice low and tense. I nod my thanks. I'm used to our enforcer's gruff demeanor and think nothing of it, as I know it's not personal. I don't know much about him. Hell, no one really does, but he's proved himself around here.

Not sure who'd be asking for me; it's not like I have regular visitors. It's been days since the accident, so I'm no longer expecting to see the sweet little thing I wrecked into show up around here. I won't lie; I'd hoped Savannah would stop through like I'd told her to, but she never did. Yesterday I'd figured that she was probably trying to stay the hell away from me. She'd seen me beating the shit outta my headlight before I dented up her car and was knocked unconscious. I must've scared her, and I can't say I blame her for keeping the distance. If I was in her shoes, I'd probably be doing the same.

Prez flashes me a look on my way out, silently asking who the fuck is coming around. I shrug, not sure what to tell him. We're not exactly keen on people sniffing around, especially with all the shit we've gone through cleaning up his father's messes. I get why he's asking. I would be too. I toss my empty Sprite bottle in the trash and take comfort in my weapon, weighing down my holster. I've had to shoot my share of twisted fucks. Still, hopefully, this isn't another one who'll be taking a bullet courtesy of my forty-five. Although, North said it's a woman, so I doubt it.

My mouth drops as I hit the parking area and notice who's waiting there. It's the innocent angel from my wreck…she finally showed after all. I've been referring to her as that in my mind the entire time. When I'd gained consciousness, she was right there, leaning over me, stars twinkling behind her, and I swear to God, I thought she was an angel come to collect my soul. Now that I think of it, I know better than to believe I'd be headed upward. My ass will be dragged straight down to the deep depths of Hell when I finally meet the reaper.

Savannah was a beautiful sobbing mess that night last week, as tears had soaked her creamy flesh. She'd smelled like delicious fried food, too; she was still in her uniform from work. I'm surprised I remember that much. Usually, I'm too busy cataloging tits and ass to see if they'd be decent prospects for Centerfolds or to dip my dick into. With this woman, I can't seem to go there, to disrespect her like that. She's a fucking angel, and anyone treating her differently deserves a swift kick to the throat. She's far too sweet to deal with the bullshit that I'm sure she often receives, with how docile and naive she appears to be.

"Sweet Pea?" I greet with one of the nicknames I'd come up with for her, as I get closer wearing a surprised, but pleased grin. Sweet Pea and Angel are two fitting names for my little road hazard.

She blushes, tucking a long lock of hair behind her ear. She glances at her feet before meeting my eyes. "You're, uh, Bash, right?"

My smile widens as I nod and reply a bit smugly. "Last time I checked." Her rosy hue, mixed with my name on her lips, makes my fucking dick hard. She was a beautiful broken mess when I first met her, but this woman before me is absolutely stunning. The type of beautiful that'll steal your breath or make your chest ache.

"You look different."

"Oh, right, I'm missing the blood, dirt, and ruined clothes," I retort with a chuckle. "I'm not the only one who's different," I point out. Her long hair has been curled into big, fluffy waves, and she's got on a light blue sundress. Doesn't she know that coming here, looking sweet as a fucking Georgia peach, is tempting the very devil in front of her? I flick my gaze from her perfectly layered curls down to her pale pink painted toes and black flip-flops. "You clean up well…really well." *I've got to figure out a way to see more of her, that I'm certain of.*

She bites her bottom lip, interest reflecting back at me. I've pegged it in many women's gazes, and hers is wide open for me to interpret. "You're not so bad yourself."

"Was that a compliment, Sweet Pea? You flirting, babe?" I tease, repeating the same question she'd asked me as I'd complimented her, half out of it from wrecking.

She shrugs, drawing in a quick breath. "Take it however you want to. I came to bring you this." She holds her dainty hand toward me. There are two twenties folded in her palm.

My brow raises as confusion fills me. "What's that for?" *Is she expecting to pay me for tightening her battery cable?*

Chicks only offer me money for one reason, and it's because they're tweaking, looking for drugs. Savannah doesn't strike me as the type wanting to score some blow. It's probably one of the reasons why I find her so unbelievably sexy. A bitch with her shit together is hot as all hell. Sure, she was freaked out when I wrecked. That's understandable, but this woman already admitted to me she's doing everything she can to pay her bills and put food on her table. It's too easy for people to just jack off and not care. She tries, and I respect her for it.

"Your motorcycle. I don't have much…but I promise to give you any extra money I do have. I think I can bring you twenty each day. If my tips are better, then more."

I can tell by the way she fidgets that she's embarrassed by this. She needn't be. I know she can't make much money working around here on the outskirts of Atlanta. Especially not at that little diner down the road. The place is usually full of coffee drinkers, not hefty tippers. Big money is in the city, and that's a decent drive from here, depending on how far you gotta go and what the traffic looks like. Besides, I'd rather take repayment in other, more creative ways. "Angel, you have any idea how much my bike cost? Or how much cash I'd need to replace it, for that matter?"

She shakes her head, looking every bit the part of an innocent Southern belle. I want to eat her up—all of her. I'm not so sure she'd survive me, but that doesn't mean I won't at least try.

"Think around twenty thousand or so…five or ten more, if I walk away with the brand-new model and no miles on it."

Her perfect, pouty lips part as she gasps with surprise. "Twenty to twenty-five or thirty thousand dollars?"

Nodding, I latch my stare onto the two bills in her hand and say, "You'd be paying me for years, beautiful. I don't want to take your money."

"Why not? What's wrong with my money?"

My lips tilt into their signature smile as I remark, "Not a damn thing, but I'd like something more." Her feistiness gives me hope that she wouldn't wither under my touch. I wonder if she's ever had it rough. Nah, fuck that, I don't want to think of her with anyone else.

She inhales a deep breath, anticipation filling her as she waits for my request. This girl is all nerves, and she has no reason to be. Could it be possible that she doesn't grasp entirely just how alluring she is to a man like me? It'd be my lucky day if that's the case. She's way out of my league, no doubt, but I'm not one to back away from something I want. Here and now, that's her.

"I'm not trying to pimp you out. It's far simpler than that." Her shoulders drop with my chuckle and reassurance. I continue. "Each time you want to bring me money, we have lunch together instead. Hell, we can just chat if you're not hungry." Not only am I doing this to secure time with her, but my guess is that she doesn't have money to go out with. This way, I don't have to eat alone or with my brothers every damn day, and I know she's fed as well. Not to mention the perks of breaking down her walls and eventually fucking her. I'm a man. Pussy is always on my mind, even if I attempt to push it toward the back to be respectful. I was already caught up with her last week on the side of the road, but seeing her like this, I'm pretty much enraptured.

"Why would you want to have lunch with me?" Her hands go to her hips. I have no doubt in my mind that this bitch is used to being independent, and with her questions, it tells me she's used to being the only one taking care of herself. Little spitfire just grows spicier by the moment.

I shrug, moving a step closer. My finger lightly presses under her chin, tipping her head up. She's fucking magnificent, a breath of fresh air around here. "If I tell you it's because I'm a man and you're a beautiful woman, would it be enough? Or would it have you turning heel and running as far from me as possible?"

Her hazel orbs take in my features, studying my face, for what, I haven't the faintest idea. Lord knows it's not the face of an honest man. My request and internal thoughts aren't good intentioned or pure. It's quite the opposite. I want her naked, bared to me, and sweaty in my bed, screaming my name while I bury my face between her thighs. If I have to come up with a way to eventually break down her walls and get her there, then so be it. I'll do what I have to. I always have.

She gives in after damn near making me break a sweat in anticipation. "Okay, I can do that. It's the least I owe you after everything."

Right. I'll let her believe she's obligated to me for as long as possible if it means I get a chance with her. It's fucked up, I know. It was my fault that my light wasn't working on that black night. The stupid headlamp had been messing up for the longest time, yet she thinks her car being in the road is the reason for my crash. I like having her in my debt; or, at least, believing she is.

My thumb lightly trails along her chin. I step back, putting much-needed distance between us before I do something stupid, like attempt to kiss her already. That'd definitely scare her off. The skittish thing doesn't seem to be used to men like me. I can't believe she had the guts to show up for me around a bunch of unruly bikers at the club in the first place. And dressed like that, to boot. She may come off as a bit naïve, but there's obviously some courage and strong will in her somewhere, leading her wherever she sees fit. Knowing that makes her even more enticing.

Fuck, I'm going to be in over my head with this one. I can already tell.

"So, what're we having for lunch then?" I murmur, and she scrambles a bit.

"Right now?"

I nod. "You brought money, and I'm not about to allow you to waste a dress like that."

Her lips tilt into a surprised smile. She allows a glimpse of her white teeth to show before she manages to tuck that extra bit of sweetness away.

Yep, I see you.

Grabbing her hand, I give it a light tug in the direction of mine and my brothers' bikes.

"Where are you taking me?"

"For a ride, Sweet Pea. I'm testing this new motorcycle out, and I have a feeling it'd help me decide to keep it or not if you were on it with me. We can stop and eat on the way…"

I don't give a fuck about food right now, to be honest. I want her curvy little body pressed against mine, and her arms wrapped tightly around me. I want to hear her scream while the wind is in her hair, and make her feel like she's flying. I wonder if she's ever been with a man as free as me. Fuck, there I go again! The last thing I need to think about is another man touching her. Hell, if I don't stop, I may end up pulling over and finger fucking her until she begs for my cock. That's not the impression I'm going for today, although I wouldn't fight it if she were to ask for it.

I turn on some Tom Petty and crank the engine once Savannah's exactly where I want her, pushed up against my back. The petite, luscious woman wraps her arms around me, tightly holding on as I toe the kickstand up. The breeze allows me to catch hints of her scent, and whatever she's got on has me gritting my teeth. The angel smells so fucking good, like sunshine and tight, clean pussy. My cock pulses in response, but it's no use. The prick won't get anything but my hand or a piece of sweetbutt ass and neither sound appealing when I have this perfect creature up against me.

I make my way out of the MC lot, but it's not lost on me that I have the attention of every brother. Amusement fills their stares as I hit the gas, and Savannah's dress goes flying. I guess I should've warned her about that happening, but I conveniently forgot. She squeals in surprise, and my laugh grows deeper. The moves combine, and my ribs scream in pain with them. I try to ignore it, to act like I'm fine, but it fucking hurts. Riding alone is painful, but adding in these antics only increases the pain level.

I roll slow for a beat, giving her a chance to tuck the fabric under her thighs. Once her other hand is back in place on my abs, I gun it again. I'd bet good money this is the first time she's been on the back of a bike, and the knowledge has my alpha silently beating his chest. I need to make sure she never forgets it—or me, for that matter.

Bash

Chapter 3

A wise girl knows her limits, a smart girl knows she has none.

- Marilyn Monroe

Savannah

Bash is crazy. The man seriously loves speed, and while I was terrified riding on the back of his fancy new motorcycle, I was also completely enthralled. I can certainly see the allure of why these men ride around like fanatics and love their motorcycles so much.

We stopped off on the side of the road, and he asked if I like barbecue. I replied by asking him if the pope was Catholic, and I watched his smile blossom. It was one of the best times I've had in a while, and we didn't even talk much. I had no idea what to say to him, and I didn't want to risk sounding like a fool. I kept wanting to apologize for the accident, but something inside told me that's not what he wanted to hear. It was great being at a random place, too, because there weren't many people around.

We sat at a picnic table and ate a tasty meal, feeling each other out a bit by staying on easy subjects. I talked a little about work and the humidity, and Bash was polite enough to not pressure me for more. I was already on edge being alone with him, as I haven't dated since before my father was killed. Bash sat back and followed my lead on the conversation, so I ended up enjoying myself more than I'd anticipated. Once we were stuffed full of delicious, tender barbecue, he brought me back to my car without hesitation. The lunch date was short, yet kinda perfect. *Was it a date? Is that what I'm considering it? Maybe.*

Bash even offered to check my car and tightened my battery cable in place again. Now I'm stuck at work filled with thoughts of him from yesterday, and I don't really know jack squat about this guy. However, one thing's for certain…he's caught my attention. There's no use trying to deny it when I can't stop myself from thinking of seeing him again—as soon as possible, preferably.

"Hey, Mary Ellen?"

"Yeah, sweetie?" The older waitress replies, turning to me as she marries ketchups. She's got fluffy, short hair, the kind that sticks up a good three inches off her scalp, and you can sort of see through it. I couldn't imagine her with any other style, however. She's got kind, deep brown eyes and one heck of a Southern drawl. She may as well be made of honey with how slow her words are, and ginormous boobs. She was no doubt part of the Dolly Parton era of women who wear bright pink lipstick religiously.

I continue to wipe down the sticky Coke machine, leaving the little nozzles on until closing. I'll have to unscrew them and pop them in a pitcher of warm water later to soak. "Do you know anything about the Kings of Carnage MC?"

Her hand flutters to her chest, the other gripping the ketchup bottle tightly. We still have the old-fashioned glass bottles rather than the smooth plastic squeezable kind. "I've heard stories. None of them appealing, I'll tell you that much."

"Have you ever met any of them, though? They seem fairly young for guys devoted to a club like that."

"I've served a couple of them coffee before, but I don't actually know them. The older members—years back—weren't the kindest of men.

They terrorized one of the local mechanics, drove him straight out of town. There have also been rumors that they'd kidnap and sell young girls. They were into all sorts of horrendous things. Supposedly, the son has taken over, and there hasn't been much said about them since then. Probably why they look young to you. That boy should be in his late twenties or somewhere around there. I'd bet the rest of them aren't far off from there."

"Oh, wow, younger than I thought."

"Yep." She nods, her brow pinched with worry. "You haven't had a run-in with them, have you? Nice girl like you; it wouldn't do you any favors, if so."

I shrug, no longer wanting to talk about Bash. He's confident and intimidating, sure, but I couldn't imagine him being ugly enough to someone it'd make them leave town. Or even worse, being involved with human trafficking. He seemed the opposite, actually; thoughtful and willing to lend a helping hand on both occasions I was around him. I have a feeling Mary Ellen likes her gossip a little too much to weave out the truth in hearsay.

"What happened, Savannah? Did one of those bikers harass you, honey?"

"Oh, no, nothing exciting like that. I had lunch with one of them yesterday, and he was really nice. That's all. I was just wondering if you knew anything more about him. I'm not too concerned, though. Like I said, he was decent."

She bursts out, "Oh, dear, thank heavens he didn't hurt you, honey! I'm afraid no one will go up against that club…not even the law. They have a rough reputation. I'm not so sure dating one of them would be a smart idea. I'd hate to see something happen to you. Who knows if they could make you disappear or not. Bad enough they're affiliated with the strip club. You know, the one that sells all that liquor? God can't be happy over that place full of sinners. Last I heard, Margret Thatcher was going to bring over some brochures from the church, hoping to reach some of those women."

"Disappear?" I repeat, my heart skipping a beat as I get stuck on that one word.

"Wouldn't put it past them," she says quietly and goes back to pouring ketchup from one bottle to fill the other. I can still hear her mumbling to herself. She's reciting some sort of prayer as she works.

"I'll be careful," I whisper and head for the bathroom.

I need a moment to myself to process what she's implied and decide if I think I can handle it. This wouldn't be my first run-in with a bad batch of men. My father was murdered for heaven's sake. While human trafficking is at the top of the list, the guys who killed my dad would be high up on there as well. The worst part of all is, I don't know why my father was murdered in the first place. One day he was here, and the next day he was gone—forever. In the beginning, I couldn't believe he was dead. It felt surreal. Eventually, the reality sank in, and the grief came crashing down along with it. My dad was an amazing guy, and his loss completely devastated me.

I hadn't given much thought to dating anyone. I've been so caught up in my own head, that no one has captured my interest. Until now, anyhow. Bash certainly made a lasting impression on me. I guess meeting over a traumatic experience will do that to you, though, where you instantly forge a type of bond. Maybe that's why I feel so comfortable around the man. Well, I'm nervous, but he doesn't intimidate me as, I'm assuming, he does to most. If the club and the guys in it are terrible like my coworker implied, then Bash has to be pretty twisted, I'd imagine, to hold the spot of vice president. I took in his patches closely yesterday, trying to figure out what half of them could mean. I didn't ask, and I won't…until we know each other better. But now, my curiosity is skyrocketing.

I'd almost eagerly made a deal with Bash that we'd have lunch together instead of me paying him. I plan to stick with my word. I told him I'd find a way to prove to him that it means something. I completely ruined his expensive motorcycle, and eating lunch with him is the least I can do—whether he's scary to some people or not. I don't think he is, but rather, he's handsome and a bit flirty. Lord knows I can't spend years attempting to pay him back at this rate, and I'm not so sure he'd be too keen on that scenario either. Maybe this all happened for some odd reason that I can't explain right now like it was fate. This man came into my life unexpectedly, and I have to find out why. I just hope it's not to end up selling me to some sex trafficker.

"Savannah Mae?" My name's called through the bathroom door, and I shut the water off. It'd been running the entire time I stood there staring in the mirror thinking of Bash. I meant to wash my hands and face, something to break up the thoughts of Bash, but I ended up getting sucked further into them. Somehow that doesn't surprise me, I'm sure it's easy getting drawn into all things that have to do with the sexy outlaw MC member.

I clear my throat, replying stronger than before. "Sorry, Mary Ellen, I'll be right out."

"Okay, sweetheart. Speaking of those bikers, you were just asking me about…"

I crack the door, peeking at her through the few inches of space. "Yes, ma'am?"

She leans in and whispers conspiratorially. "One of them just came in, asking for a to-go order."

My eyes widen, and I inhale deeply. I step out into the tiny hallway that leads from the restrooms back into the small diner. I can't help but wonder, or to hope, "W-was it Bash?"

"Says his name is Sly. I didn't ask for anything else. Not trying to have trouble pointed in my direction if you know what I mean."

Swallowing, I nod. "All right, then. Let's get out there before he thinks anything of us being back here for too long."

She follows along, and as we step out of the hallway, I see the man she'd mentioned. It'd be hard not to miss him. Not only is he the only guy in here, but he's gorgeous. He's got short hair and a closely-cut beard to match; both are dark. His scruff reminds me of Bash's. That's not what sticks out the most, though…it's the ink on his neck and left arm. The artwork is beautiful. Mary Ellen and I go behind the counter to our station, and the biker glances up. I briefly meet his light green stare, the color reminding me of a Granny Smith apple and offer a friendly smile.

"Do you need to-go silverware or any extra sauces with your order?" I ask as Mary Ellen skedaddles back over to her condiments, keeping to herself. She's probably thrilled I've questioned the biker if he needs anything, so she doesn't have to extend that courtesy.

"Mayo and ketchup. Can't keep either around with the brothers always eating my shit." He's not rude or grouchy. Sly's the opposite, actually, and I find myself smiling wider. Is it just a coincidence that I'd never see any of these bikers in here, and the day after I have lunch with Bash, another just happens to walk into the diner I work at?

"Not a problem. I'll make sure to put some in with your food order."

"Appreciate that." He nods.

"You want something to drink while you wait?"

"I'm fine," he replies.

I step closer to the food window. Grabbing the order ticket Mary Ellen wrote up, I check it over and notice that this isn't just Sly's food. I quickly place the ticket back in its spot—the cook gets pissed if we move them. It looks like several of Bash's brothers put in an order for food as well. Could Bash have been the one to send Sly in for food? It'd have to be him, right? Noticing how many meals he's taking back, I grab an empty bag and fill it half full of ketchup and mayo packets, along with some napkins. I've seen plenty of men eat before. They manage to get messy even if it's just an order of french fries on their plate.

"Orders up!" Sam calls loudly, and I head back to the window. There're about twelve to-go boxes stacked up next to each other in the small area.

"Thanks, Sam," I say and take the Styrofoam containers down to place in multiple plastic bags. Sly's already paid, so I set the seven bags down on the counter in front of him. "Would you like some help carrying all this to your vehicle?" I'm hoping he didn't ride his motorcycle. That'd be a little awkward trying to get all this food to stay in one place and warm. Just the fact he's picking up their own food has me a bit stunned. Door

Dash has pretty much taken over the bulk of to-go orders, even out here away from the city.

"Would you mind that, doll? I don't want to put you out or anything. I can make a few trips, though. Don't want to fuck up our grub." He grabs four of the bags, leaving me three and the condiment bag.

"It's no trouble at all." I grab the others and follow his lead. He stops at a big truck parked out front and loads the food into the passenger side. I hand over the other bags and go to head back inside.

He stops me, saying, "Your tip, doll."

"Oh, thank you!" I flash a surprised, grateful smile as Sly hands some cash over. I take it without looking, thinking it's a dollar or two, same as my other tips during the day. Most of the people stopping in are coffee drinkers and sandwich eaters, so I don't make much. Sundays are the best days for tips with the church crowd, and I rarely get lucky enough to have that shift. He grins, walking around the truck and offers me a salute as he slides in behind the wheel. The handsome tatted man pulls away, and I nearly pinch myself as it doesn't feel real. At another time, if I hadn't already met Bash, I'd be asking all about Sly.

I step back inside, opening my palm to stuff the cash into my apron. As I glance down, not paying it much mind, I see that it's not only a dollar bill but a twenty. For all the negative things Mary Ellen had to say about the Kings of Carnage guys, so far, none of it seems like it could be true. Not even close. The two members I've come across have been somewhat polite and friendly, and both of them have helped me in different ways. Bash helped with my broken-down car, and now Sly has helped by giving me a big tip without asking for anything in return. Granted, his bill couldn't have been cheap with all the food he ordered, but it was a to-go order, and around here, people barely tip anything when they take the food with them.

"Lordy, I can't believe you went outside alone with him!" the older woman chastises as I flip the open sign on the door to closed and turn the lock, then head for the soda machine. I can finally finish. We've been so freaking slow today, I have practically everything done already, so I can leave right away. I'm exhausted from being on my feet all dang day and want to get back to my shithole apartment to relax. This stress is killing me.

"He was a perfect gentleman. I'm sure you watched the entire exchange."

Her cheeks pink a bit as she stacks the bottles under the counter. She'd finally finished filling them and wiping everything down. "Well, I wasn't going to let you get kidnapped without calling in the law."

I chuckle, shaking my head at her overreaction. What would Mary Ellen think if she knew everything about me? She'd probably lump me into the same category she has the bikers and write me off completely. I want to tell her not to waste her time calling the cops for me—ever. It'd probably only do more harm than good, in my case. I'm not going to, however. Knowing her, she'd be gossiping about me next.

"Thanks for your concern, but I survived." I flash a fake smile in her direction. I don't know why her opinions and reactions toward the bikers piss me off so much, but they do. Maybe because I've seen firsthand how they treat me, and it was nothing like she'd referred to.

"I'm out of here," I call loudly enough so Sam can hear me as well. They both chime in with their goodbyes, and I grab my purse from under the counter. I head out the front door and off to the side parking lot where I always park my hatchback. Wrenching the door open, I hop in, exhaling in relief that my day is over, and I don't have to deal with any more people. I toss my purse into the passenger seat along with my rolled-up apron and stick the key into my ignition.

The hunk of junk doesn't start when I turn it over. I do what any sane woman in my position would. I scream at the steering wheel and then hold my breath as I attempt to get the stubborn car to start again. It doesn't work, and there's still no response when I turn the key. I sit, pondering what my options are for a few minutes, but there's not much more I can do. I need to call for a ride home and worry about this car in the morning when it's not night time and I'm alone out here without any idea on how to fix the damn car. With an angry glower, I grab my shit and hurry back to the restaurant's front door. Mary Ellen already locked it up, so I beat on the window, hoping someone's still inside. It's no use. She and Sam left out the back door, probably right after I did.

Near tears, I sit on the curb outside the restaurant's front door. The past few months have been hard on me, but there's nothing I can do to change that. I have a feeling it's only going to get worse at this rate. There's a streetlamp over here, so it doesn't seem quite as creepy as the parking lot.

A truck pulls to stop on the curb. The window rolls down, and Sly's handsome face pops out. "You okay?"

I shake my head. Not in the slightest, but I don't admit it to him. "I need to use the phone and the restaurant's locked up."

He holds his hand out his window with his cell. "You can use mine, anytime, just ask."

I jump up, coming closer. "Thanks." It's one of those cheap prepaid phones like my own that has no minutes. I ask, "Do you happen to know the number for a cab or an Uber?"

He shakes his head, flicking his verdant gaze from my toes up to my own hazel orbs. "If you need a ride, hop in. It was luck or something; I had to stop by Mooney's Pub before heading back to the club. Glad I did, or you may've been stuck here all night."

I know what he means. We're on the outskirts of Atlanta, and there's not a lot around unless you get closer to the city. "I appreciate the offer, and while you seem nice, I can't get into a truck with a man I don't know."

"Isn't Uber basically the same thing?"

"Yeah, but it's their job," I argue, attempting to be rational.

"It really is your lucky night," he mutters cryptically and hits some buttons on his cell before putting it to his ear. The other person picks up as he begins speaking into the phone. "Brother? Yeah. Found your angel on the curb outside the diner."

A moment later, Sly looks to me, asking, "Your car break again?"

I nod.

He speaks back to the person on the phone. "Yep, it's fucked. All right, I'll let her know." He hangs up and meets my curious stare. "Bash said to sit tight; he's on his way."

"What? No. He doesn't need to come here. I'm fine, really."

He snorts and digs into one of the bags I put in his truck. He comes back with a handful of fries that he stuffs into his mouth. He just watches me and eats.

"What are you doing?" I ask after observing him eat all of his fries.

"I'm waiting for my brother. Bash is on his way, and if I'm not here keeping an eye on your safety, he'll be pissed the fuck off. Not trying to deal with my brother and his short fuse. The motherfucker is called Bash for a reason, and I like to hit back." He winks with that last little detail.

Holy shit, it's been a little over a week since I came across these guys, and suddenly, they're everywhere. And why on earth doesn't that bother me? No matter what I do, I can't seem to get Bash off my mind. Knowing I'll be straddling him has me squeezing my legs together. I've attempted to ward off the ever-present ache that's been there since he took me for a ride yesterday at lunch. *I mean, straddling his bike…not him. Oops.*

Chapter 4

I'm not crazy, my reality is just different from others.

- Alice in Wonderland

Bash

I'm shocked that Sly hit me up, letting me know that Angel's car is leaving her stranded again. How he was around long enough to find out is beyond me. I just fixed the damn battery cable yesterday. I made sure to tighten it enough so it wouldn't pop off again. I have a feeling this is the beginning of a downward spiral of her car taking a shit on her for good. Luckily for Savannah, I know my way around old ass vehicles like her hatchback. If it were some new model, she'd really be screwed because I haven't the slightest clue about the computers and what not they shove inside them nowadays.

I'd filled my brothers in on my wreck last week. I let them know how Savannah didn't hesitate to make sure I was all right. I had to bring them up on the details since my bike was totaled, and I needed a ride to check it out and get it towed. Then yesterday, they saw Sweet Pea come to the clubhouse and ride off with me to lunch. Today, I'd asked Sly to specifically hit up the small diner and get us something to munch on before we party tonight. I figured it'd be a good way to check in on her without actually being there and also hooking her up with some extra cash. I know she needs it, even if she'd never admit it. I'm glad he took my suggestion and stopped by, or Savannah could've ended up stranded or hitchhiking home without anyone knowing about it.

She seriously needs to get her fucking phone back. At least then I can make sure she has my number programmed so she can hit me up if she ever needs anything. I may have let her believe that she's in debt to me because my motorcycle was totaled in the wreck, but that's not the reality of it. The truth of the matter is, anyone could've left me on the side of the road and split. Or else not given a flying fuck whether I was still breathin' or had met the reaper. Savannah stuck by my side, sobbing her eyes out, praying I was okay. When I saw that angel holding me like I was the most precious fucking thing to her, I knew I had to find a way to be in her life. Obviously, this is the way I'm going to do it. At least until she gives in to my charm and allows me to put her fine ass in my bed.

I pull my new motorcycle to a stop behind my brother's truck, my body still aching from the wreck. Dropping the kickstand in place, I swing my leg over, breathing through the sharp pain slicing through me and offer Savannah a grin. I wanted to see her so fucking bad today, and I ended up getting a chance. It looks like fate was on my side again.

"Brother," I greet Sly. His truck smells amazing—like french fries—and it causes my stomach to grumble from hunger.

He flashes me an amused grin. "You want your grub now, or you holding off?"

"I'll wait. Appreciate you sticking around with Angel."

He bobs his nearly shaved head and mutters, "I was on my way back from stopping by the pub. Glad I caught her." He must've been out collecting protection money for the MC. It's one of his responsibilities. I've gone with him before on a few collections. It was a little too dull for me, so I stick to what I do best. I maintain our drug relationships and distribution. The Kings of Carnage has many lucrative business ventures; mine happens to lie in drugs.

"Me too. I'll catch up with you at the clubhouse." I chin-lift his way, and he returns the notion, pulling away from the curb.

I turn around, finding the gorgeous spitfire watching me curiously. "Hey, Sweet Pea, you straight?"

Her lips tilt up. She's pleased to see me, even if she attempts to play it cool. I can read it all over that perfect, pouty mouth of hers. Those lips were made to do more than just talk, there's not a doubt in my mind. "I'm never going to stop owing you if you keep helping me out. I'm always stranded around you, it appears."

I wave her comment off. "This is what friends do, yeah? You helped me when I needed it, now I do the same for you."

She releases a nervous breath, and I hold out a hand. She takes it, allowing me to help her to her feet. "Thanks, Bash, I really don't know what I'd do without you and your friend."

"Sly."

She nods, "Yeah, he was nice enough to let me use his phone when I asked, but then he took it right back. He wasn't going to have me call for an Uber. He said you'd want to know and would be on your way. Are you guys always like this with people needing a hand?"

"He's right. I did want to come get you and consider yourself an exception to our usual attitude toward civilians." I tug her closer, noticing the goosebumps peppering the creamy skin on her arm. "You cold?"

She shrugs. "I'll live. It could be worse; I could be stuck out here alone and cold."

I grunt, heading over to my saddlebag. I put a hoodie in there last night after I finished signing the paperwork for my new motorcycle. It was chilly last night, too, so I'm glad I left it in here. After having Savannah on the bike, it was a done deal. I had to have it, as it would always remind me of her first ride and her dress flying high to flash my brothers.

I fold up the shirt in my hands until I have the head opening between my grip and pop it over Savannah's silky hair.

"You didn't have to do that," she argues, blowing the locks out of her face and making me chuckle.

"I want to. Now put it on the rest of the way, Sweet Pea." She does as she's told, and fuck me if she doesn't look hella sexy all wrapped up in my big shirt. It falls mid-thigh on her, and the KOCMC emblem across the front makes her look every bit mine. She pulls the collar up to her nose, taking a deep inhale. "Probably smells like exhaust, sorry about that."

She shakes her head. "It does a little, but I still smell you in it. Plus, it's warm, so that trumps exhaust scent any day."

I chuckle and lean in a touch closer. "You know how I smell, hm?"

She nods, biting down on her perfectly plump bottom lip. "I held on to you yesterday, remember? I had no choice but to sniff you being that close."

"Mm. I couldn't forget it if I tried beautiful. How about you hop on and hold onto me some more?"

"I'd like that," she agrees with a soft smile, and I turn away, leading her to my bike.

I swing my leg over, getting comfortable. "We're having a party tonight at the club. How about you come with me and cut loose?" I suggest, holding her hand as she climbs on my bike, placing her feet on the back pegs.

She yawns. "I'm sure you guys are a lot of fun, but I'm so tired. I had to work all day, and I really want to go to bed." Her hands land on my sides, sliding against my shirt until they reach my abs. I cringe to myself with the soreness but suck it up. It's what I've been doing since she showed up yesterday, pretending my ribs aren't bothering me anymore. I walk the bike forward, and the move has me clenching my stomach and gritting my teeth. Aside from soreness still in my bones, my desire for her is fucking fierce, and it only increases with every touch I receive from her.

"It's a shame, babe. Would've liked seeing you chill with me." I crank the engine, noting how she scoots as close as possible to my back. She must've learned to duck in and hold on from yesterday.

"Rain check?" she calls over my shoulder, and my mood lifts with her suggestion. Hell, I'll throw another party myself, just to get her ass out with me.

"Of course. Anytime, and I mean that." I pull from the curb, asking loudly, "Am I going in the right direction?"

"Yes. I live in those brown apartments down the road from your club."

"No shit?"

"Yeah, why?"

"I live there too."

"Seriously?"

I nod and holler, "Hold on." I turn up the radio, allowing "Enter Sandman" by Metallica to blare loudly. We hit the dark, deserted stretch of road the club's on, and I gun it, concentrating on the road ahead of us. What are the odds the woman of my most recent fantasies lives in the same apartment complex that I do? Granted, I'm not there much, and we must not live on the same side, because I know there's no way in hell I ever could've missed her being a neighbor. The angel takes my breath away and makes my cock tingly in the best sort of way whenever she's around.

With the wind raking through our hair, I enjoy the cool night air on our short ride. The best part is having her snuggled up to my back. I wish she would've been open to partying tonight, but at least I got her to offer me a rain check. Maybe it's not her scene.

Hell, I need a drink something fierce with how bad I've been aching. I love a stiff vodka tonic and enjoy getting my dick wet at our parties. The crazy nights are part of what drew me into the MC, aside from Chaos, my prez. He's become my best friend over the years, the brother I can rely on the most. I've been by his side for too long now to imagine changing my way of life. The club is everything to me, and I hope that's not a deal-breaker for the spicy Southern belle on the back of my ride.

Turning into the apartments, Savannah points to the left, directing me to her place in the front of the building. It figures that I was right about her being on opposite sides. My spot is to the right, tucked around the complex. It offers me more privacy, which is what I prefer, being associated with the MC. You never know when a rival or disgruntled dickhead may see where you live and seek some retribution. It doesn't bother me when I'm at the club, knowing my brothers are all around me to help watch my back. At home, though, I like to sleep at night, not worrying I'll be gunned down at two a.m. for whoever I recently rubbed wrong.

"This is it," she instructs, and I pull up to the curb.

Kicking my stand down, I climb off, then hold my palm out to her and grab my bike with my free hand. She takes the offering, allowing me to help her off. "Careful of the pipes, Sweet Pea. Just like yesterday," I remind, and she offers me a sweet smile. *The bitch is fucking beautiful.* She doesn't drop my hand as I allow her to lead me to her door.

"This one's mine." She thumbs in the direction of the blue door. It's not navy, nor pastel, just a medium blue that's been painted on all of our doors when the owners attempted to freshen them up and bring in more tenants.

My head bobs. "I'm in six-oh-five around the back. If you ever need anything, you hit me up, 'kay, babe?"

"Thank you, Bash."

"It's Sebastian."

"Excuse me?"

I stand a bit taller, my back straightening and chest-puffing as I confess, "My name…it's Sebastian. You can keep callin' me Bash or Seb or Sebastian…whatever you feel comfortable with."

She rewards me with a wide smile. "Sebastian," she repeats, tasting the word over before claiming, "I like it."

My mouth kicks up. "Yeah? It'd be a little awkward if you felt differently, 'cause I like your name too."

She nods, and I can no longer hold myself back from leaning in to press a peck to her pointy little nose. Bitches pay for noses like hers, and I can tell that not one thing on her is fake.

"And I also like you, Angel." She blushes, her eyes hitting the ground. "I'm up here, Savannah," I murmur, reaching in to tilt her face back up. I meet her gaze, noting the desire reflected in her gorgeous hazel irises. *Fuck, I want her.*

"I see you," she whispers.

"Do you?" I murmur, and she nods again. I step back, flashing her a smile. I don't want to push her too hard. "I mean it. Anything."

"Are you going by the diner tomorrow?"

"Yes," I immediately lie. I wasn't, but I damn sure am now that she's brought it up.

"If you wouldn't mind, would you give me a ride too?"

"Of course. What time, and I'll swing by to pick you up."

"My shift is at two. I have to work the dinner shift again."

"It's a date." I wink and head for my bike. I swing my leg on, starting the beast up. I let the engine idle as I watch her get inside safely. Once her door's securely closed, I walk my bike to turn it around, then hit the road, headed to my club. This time I don't even feel my ribs protesting. I'm too busy thinking of Savannah and that perfect mouth.

Sapphire Knight

"Heard you had an extra rider with you tonight, brother."

I shoot Jinx a look. "You and Sly been talkin', I take it?"

He shrugs, not perturbed in the slightest with my brusque response. "He may've mentioned it when he brought me my sandwich."

I snort and take a hefty gulp of my vodka tonic. "It was the angel, man. She was stranded again. That damn car's a piece of shit."

"You didn't fix it for her? I'm beginning to think you're not so much a mechanic." His lips tilt with the easy razzing.

"Hm, I fixed it. The stupid thing is dying, though."

"So why didn't you bring the chick along tonight? She afraid of the club or something?"

"She was beat from working all day. She was damn near sleeping standing up. Trust me, brother, I tried. The bitch is so fucking sexy. I need to get her a burner or something in case she's stranded again and needs me to swing by. Definitely don't want one of the backwoods motherfuckers swooping in on her. She'd wind up hog-tied in an old house or something crazy."

Jinx nods. The brothers know she's alluring, just as much as I do. I told the fuckers after my little lunch date with her yesterday that they better not get any ideas either. Just 'cause I had a little fun with her and flashed them doesn't mean I'm down to share. She doesn't seem that kinky anyhow, and it'd scare her off, no doubt. I don't have to worry about Chaos, but I'm not sure if the other brothers are seeing anyone significant. They haven't brought a chick around in a minute.

He changes topics. "You end up getting rid of the rest of your stash?" Jinx and I have that in common, *the drugs*. It works in our favor, cause if one of us is short or a supplier falls through, we have a backup plan. On the other side of the business, if we aren't pushing a product quickly enough, we can always go to each other for help. It gives us a reason to be closer than the others, even though I'm usually around the prez the most.

"Yeah, some rich fucks out in Atlanta hit me up, you know, the usual. It's time for me to call my guy for another shipment. How's business been on your side? Did the number I give you pan out?"

"Fuck, yes, a big payday. I owe you a beer for that one."

I lean in, bumping my fist to his. "Bet. I'm glad to hear it, brother." Sly pulls the opposite seat out beside me, some nameless club gash sidling up to his arm. No matter where we go, the bitches are always trying to cling to him. "'Sup man."

"Where's Savannah?" he inquires, making my jealousy overreact and flair. I know he won't go for her since I told them all to kick rocks, but something about her makes me turn all overbearing alpha and shit. Not that she needs it. The woman has a spine that I admire. She's not bitchy about it or anything, just not too meek to hold back if she has something she thinks is important to say. I can't help but be a touch wary around the brother when it comes to women. I mean, I'm decent looking and all, but chicks gaze at Sly like he hung the moon, and that's when he's busy ignoring them.

"She's mine, brother," I rasp, and he flashes me a shit-eating grin. "Fucker." I gripe, causing both of my brothers to chuckle. "All right, shitheads," I huff out, tired of having my dick in a wad. "I'll catch you later. I need to speak with Prez."

They nod, letting me off the hook. It won't be for long, though, as we always give each other shit.

Sapphire Knight

Chapter 5

I know my worth. I've paid dearly for every ounce of it.

- Alfa

Savannah

Sebastian had my car towed to his clubhouse, by a friend of his. All I know is they didn't ask me for any money when I was silently hyperventilating about it and that he's been trying to fix it. So far, he hasn't had any luck, and it's looking worse with each passing day. It's been over a week, though I can't complain. He's offered to check it out for free, which is more than any shop will do, considering I can't afford to pay anything right now. At this rate, I'm going to have to look for another job to help foot the bill. That's hard because I need a place that'll pay me under the table like the diner does. My boss was more than happy when I asked, as it's less tax hassle for him. I wonder if he knows of another business I could apply for since I can't pick up any more shifts at the diner. I'll have to ask him the next time he's there.

It's been a little over two weeks since I met my new biker friend, and so far, he hasn't let me shake him off. Surprising, considering I keep piling up my problems, it seems. He's been rolling right along with them, and that has me pausing to seriously consider taking another step with him. I know he wants me; the flirty remarks and kind gestures when he's around have clued me in. I'd have to be completely blind not to notice the way he stares at my breasts and behind when he thinks I'm distracted. Not like I have any room to talk. I've done my fair share of gawking at him as well. The man is insanely good-looking—in that bad boy outlaw sort of way.

To top it all off, Sebastian has been giving me a ride to work every day and picking me up in the evenings as well. That's something I wasn't expecting in the slightest and tried fighting him on after the second day. He's done so much for me already, and I don't like feeling as if I owe him past fixing my car. Besides, I'm already in debt to him where his old motorcycle is concerned. Every time I bring it up, he shakes it off like it's not a big deal. I'm afraid that it'll all add up and he'll want something I can't give him. I've caught glimpses of the little baggies and vials of white powder and pills he pulls out when he's digging in his pockets for stuff. I'm not a fool. I know he deals, and that's not something I could ever see myself doing, no matter how much I owe someone. I'm not judging him for it. It's just not for me.

Not that I have any room to talk. I may not deal any drugs, but I have my own demons. I came to the outskirts of Atlanta for a reason, thinking I'd be easily overlooked. I work for cash under the table, so I don't leave a trail, and I bought my car with cash. I don't want people to know where I am after my father's death. He was purposely bankrupted and murdered, and I was never able to find out why it all went down. I know I'm not safe, so I have to keep a low profile. While I'm growing more comfortable around Bash and would love to have the chance to maybe become *more* with him, I need to be careful. I didn't move out here looking for my life partner. It was just the opposite. I came here for my personal safety and cash—nothing more.

I'm so torn when it comes to the MC. Those guys are dangerous, and I kind of feel safer when I'm around them. That's stupid, I know, but I can't help the way I feel, especially around my biker. I don't expect him to protect me by any means, but my heart wants to believe he would if I ever needed it, and that'd tether me to him even more. It's probably going to end up being the very thing that gets me killed. The MC could possibly have ties to the man who murdered my father, for all I know. It's not like I can come right out and ask them or anything, for fear of finding out they *are* the bad guys.

Atlanta isn't far from here. I should've gone farther away, but I haven't had the funds to make it anywhere else. The plan was to stop here long enough to work and get some more money. Once I saved up enough, I was going to leave and head up to Oregon. I figure I have a better chance of making it out of the country if I'm way up north near the border. What do I know, though? I've never been on the run or hiding out from anyone before.

Without me accidentally meeting Bash a few weeks ago, there's no telling what sort of shape I'd be in right now. I'd be walking to and from work each day, leaving me out in the open for anyone to find me. It's scary when you try to only rely on yourself. Not even my best friend could've dug me out of these problems. She makes enough money to support herself, not to give me a handout whenever things are tough.

I've always been somewhat intelligent, or so I thought, but this is turning out to be tougher than I'd anticipated. I got beyond lucky when Bash wrecked that he was okay and didn't call the cops to report it. Now my luck seems to be running out because a broken car won't get me where I need to go—work or otherwise. I could attempt to steal a vehicle, I suppose, but then the cops would hunt it down the moment it was reported and take me straight to jail. While I pride myself on being strong-willed and independent, I don't think I'd fare well in prison.

Like it or not, Bash has become some sort of rock for me. I shouldn't lean on him, and I don't want to, but I can't seem to help myself. With each passing day, I grow happier to see his handsome, smiling face. We talk, and I find myself opening to him a touch more with each encounter. It's to the point that my favorite part of the day is seeing him when I should be concentrating on making it farther away from here. Instead, I'm spending time with Bash whenever I'm offered the chance and find myself returning his flirty looks and comments. I'm a scatterbrained mess. No matter how smart I may be, my heart will lead me however it sees fit.

I wish my father were here and still alive. I wouldn't be dealing with any of this headache right now if the circumstances were different. It's astonishing how quickly your life can change from one side of the spectrum to the complete opposite. It felt like a blink to me, and bam, everything was ruined. I can still hear the officers' voices in my mind as they'd told me about my dad. It was all white noise to me…none of it making sense. My father was a thoughtful and generous man filled with love and always willing to lend a helping hand. There was no justifiable reason for him to die.

Perhaps that's why I'm drawn to Bash more than anyone else I've come across here. Minus the flirty looks and such, he reminds me of my dad in a few crucial ways. There's his willingness to help and not ask for anything in return. Then the small glimpses I've been privy to showing me that he has a fierce sense of loyalty to his brothers and his club. That has to count for something, and maybe in time, I'll be able to open up to him about my past and the burden I've been carrying around on my shoulders. It's a struggle to bear it alone, but I know I must be wary of entrusting people so quickly. My father trusted, and he ended up dead for it. If there's one lesson to be learned from this horrifying experience, it has to be that.

"Angel?" Sebastian waves his hand in front of my face, bending down a bit to catch my gaze. I was staring off into space, wrapped up in my torturous thoughts of my dad. I can't believe I lost myself like that in front of him. I was relaxing watching Bash, and in the next minute, I was trapped in my mind.

"Oh, what were you saying?" I meet his azure irises, feeling a bit shaky and thrown off-kilter. He must already believe me to be a needy loser; I don't want to add scatterbrained crazy person to that list as well.

"I asked if you're all right." His hand moves to lift my chin higher.

I'd had it tucked into my chest as I'd been immersed in my head. He does that a lot, having me meet his eyes when we talk. Not that I mind. I like it, but it also makes it harder for me to keep things from him. In another life, I like to think that I could be completely honest with him, and he'd accept me for all my flaws. Maybe he'd tell me everything would be okay and seal it with a kiss? A girl can dream about such comforts, right?

"Of course, I am. Why wouldn't I be?"

His thumb tenderly caresses my cheek. "You whimpered, *baby*. I thought you were upset, and it caught me off guard."

I swallow, my throat feeling dry suddenly. Jesus, the things this man does to me with a simple, innocent touch. My lashes flutter as I attempt to get myself together and not be so easily affected by him. We've almost kissed nearly every day this last week, and it's been freaking torture to not give in to the natural feeling. At least, I think it's natural. I don't know what it is, but something about Bash pulls me to him. "I was, uh, thinking about my father. I miss him. I miss him really bad; it hurts my heart."

His worried stare softens, and he pulls me into his chest, wrapping his strong arms around me. I've come to discover that Bash is a hugger. I didn't realize how badly I needed his embraces until they started happening a couple days ago. "I'm here if you need me. I know I'm not your dad and all, but I got you, Sweet Pea. You can talk to me about anything, at any time. Even if it's late, you know where my place is. Don't hesitate to stop over…I mean it."

A lone tear trails down my face. I can't allow myself to sob in grief like I so desperately desire to. It'll invite too much attention, and that's the last thing I need. My hands smooth over his strong middle, my grip lightly resting on his sides. Even when I'm distressed, I can't help but notice how sexy he is. He's had his ribs wrapped up since his wreck, and I've selfishly ignored the pain he must be in. He's been riding his motorcycle every day to give me rides and fixing my car. It wouldn't hurt me to offer to help him out, even if it's getting him to take it easy at times. I need to stop making everything about me when it comes to Bash because he always thinks of others. He deserves to have that as well, whether we're only friends or not.

"Thank you, Sebastian." I sigh. "That means a lot. More than you realize."

He plants a kiss to the top of my hair. Pulling away a little, he peeks down at my face and uses his thumb to wipe my warm salty tear away. "How can I make you happy? You're too beautiful to cry and me not fix it somehow."

I shrug. I can't believe what he's asking me. It's more than anyone else has done since I left my home and everything else behind. I stuffed a duffle bag full of my essentials and left the rest of my possessions behind. I had to keep my best friend safe from Jerome's family, and the easiest way to do that was to leave.

Inhaling, I manage to question, "You ever have those days when you're just sad?" Bash doesn't reply, but rather, he squeezes me to him tighter. "I think it's one of those days for me," I end up acknowledging.

"Fuck, Savannah. Honestly, I don't know if I can handle you being depressed over shit. I don't want to freak you out, but it's messing me up inside to see someone so innocent, like you, dealin' with it. I wish there was someone physically messing with you, so I could fuckin' strangle them for you, babe. It'd make it a hell of a lot easier for me to fix. You're too damn good and pure to be feeling out of sorts. It's not fucking fair. You deserve the world, sweetheart, and life's dealt you a shit hand."

His words make my heart squeeze. Some women may be put off by his violent declaration and brash words, but it does the opposite for me. This man is one of a kind, and for me to stick with my plan, I have to leave him behind and never turn back. That's becoming harder with every minute I spend in his presence. "You're so good to me, Bash. I don't understand why…I haven't done anything right to deserve you."

He lifts my chin again, this time dipping down to rub his nose to mine in an Eskimo kiss. It's the sweetest thing, and through my sadness, it brings a tender smile to my lips. "There she is…my little angel. So fucking beautiful."

I move to argue, to tell him I'm far from being an angel. I'm the opposite, in fact, and I don't deserve anything he's doing for me. Nor the way he treats me, but I don't get the chance. He dips in, his full lips finally coming in contact with mine. I've waited for weeks for this. My eyes slam closed at the sensation. I've thought of kissing him ever since he told me his name. He was lascivious and forbidden and had just gone through a small bit of hell alongside me. *I should've known I was already falling for him right then, but I was clueless.*

His mouth moves against mine, caressing, coaxing, but not forcing. He's doing this at my pace, letting me control how fast and far we take this. His lips meet mine a third time, and I exhale as desire spirals through my veins at an insane pace. Need for this man nearly consumes me, having him this close, holding me and kissing me. I want him to strip me bare and put that mouth all over me. I want him to *taste* me.

"Sebastian…" I release his name on a breathy moan, and it's all the confirmation for more that he needs. He dives in, nudging my mouth open with his own. His tongue plunges inside, searching for mine. I meet him head-on, our tongues caressing and testing the other out as our lips seal.

I take in his smell, the leather from his cut, and the grease from my car. There's a hint of exhaust leftover from our ride earlier and mixed with his soap, it smells like freedom and sweet promises. He tastes of lemon, lime, and sugar from the Sprite he was drinking earlier, and the flavors are even better on him. He cups my cheek in his palm while I move my right hand to rest over his heart. I feel it beating strong while I grip his side with my opposite hand, holding me in place. I have to grasp on somewhere, or my knees may end up giving out, with the way his kiss rolls over me and tugs me under.

I wasn't sure about Bash, but his kiss tells me so much. This man is all about giving, and I want him…*I want him bad.* I can hear myself whimper as I open my mouth wider and dive in, needing to consume him however he'll allow it. With my muted plea, his hands move to my thighs, lifting me up against the side of my car. My legs spread, allowing him to fit snugly against my core. My body's blazing all over, the sad thoughts from moments ago long forgotten. He's the only thing on my mind now, with his addictive kiss. I've wanted this since I climbed onto his bike and held him in my arms.

With a grunt, he presses his length into my clit. The sensation has me gasping, and he takes full advantage of my surprise. His tongue takes over, gaining complete control of our kiss as my focus moves to my throbbing pussy and his delightful torture. In the next beat, he's pushing my delicate teal lace panties to the side so his fingers can dip into my wetness. My drenched entrance gives me away, and he gasps in delight, thrusting a finger deep. It feels so dang good. I haven't had a man touch me in so long, and never one as irresistible as Sebastian.

"I…" I manage to puff, ripping my mouth away to breathily protest. Although my body is telling me to lie down and spread wide. "I can't have sex with you."

"No?" he growls, his pupils dilated with desire. The word is more of a taunt as he doesn't hesitate to pump into my core again, then go back in, adding a second finger. He's testing me to see if I mean it, if I can hold on to my willpower. Lord knows I don't want to. I wish I could do whatever I want, but I have to be rational, think about the potential consequences.

"Oh, Bash… Oh, geez."

"Yeah?" He tugs my earlobe between his teeth, biting down hard enough to send a shock of pain down my throat. My nipples are on full alert, begging for him to bite there next.

"I mean it. We can't have sex," I blurt out, reminding him, even though every bit of me wants to give in and allow him to take me right here. We're outside, in the open for anyone to see us. Not only that, but it's far too soon. I'm not an easy lay; I never have been.

"Good thing I'm only finger fucking you then, huh?" Another whimpering moan escapes my lips at the deep rumbling timbre of his words. "Christ, Angel, this pussy is so goddamn juicy for me. I've been dreaming of this peachy cunt, and it's more perfect than I'd imagined."

My pussy clenches at his throaty rasp and my nipples pebble, my body craving its fair share of attention in all this delicious torment. It's not going to happen, though—us getting closer—it can't. "Your touch…it feels good—real good." And that's putting it lightly.

"What does? My fingers thrusting into this tight, creamy cunt?"

"Mm." My pelvis thrusts, moving with his hand as my orgasm swiftly builds into something intense and divine. He pushes in, especially deep, and my toes curl. It feels so damn amazing. "Faster," I hiss, and he immediately speeds up, pumping two fingers in and out repeatedly.

"I'd add another finger, but, baby, this pussy is so fuckin' tight. I don't wanna hurt you. Christ, when I do stick my cock in you—and before you argue about it, you better realize it's gonna fucking happen, I promise you that much. But, when I do get in this warm, wet cunt, my cock's gonna stretch you so fuckin' good, it'll make you scream my name. You'll want more. *That,* I can promise you."

His words send me over. My forehead hits his shoulder, and my pussy squeezes his fingers as tightly as possible. My mouth falls open as my juices down below gush out, leaking all over his hand and my ass crack. He continues to pump them, allowing me to work through every last second of my blissful orgasm.

"Goddamn," he curses quietly. "Damn." I open my eyes with my mouth parted, expelling soft pants as I meet his blazing cerulean stare. Jesus, I don't know if I've ever witnessed a man with me look as turned on as he does. His skin is flushed, his nostrils flaring as he breathes me in. "You're the most beautiful woman I've ever seen, Angel. Swear it on my life."

His compliment has me tilting my head a bit to gaze at him through my lashes. The feeling is completely mutual. He's gorgeous. I can't believe I just let myself go like that with him—out here. It's reckless, and not like me, but I'm not the least bit sorry for it. That orgasm was intense, and I needed it more than I realized.

He pulls his wet, sticky fingers free, and I slowly slide back down off his hips to plant my feet on the gravel. I can't turn away, watching as he sticks the two fingers from my pussy into his mouth. He sucks, emitting a long, intense groan. His eyes flutter closed as he savors my taste before removing them to compliment, "So sweet."

My lips lift into a smile, and I bite my bottom lip. I admit, "That was a little crazy."

He drops his fingers, flashing me a grin. "Nah, Sweet Pea, that was merely an appetizer."

"That so?" A giggle escapes me, and my eyes go wide as he goes to his knees before me. "W-what are you doing?" I whisper-shout, floored by his spontaneous actions.

Sebastian flashes me that smug smile of his that reels me in and ducks his head under my dress. It's a loose, knee-length sundress that surprisingly has enough stretch so he can easily fit underneath. He draws in a deep breath, nose pressed against my core. His hot breath hits me as he exhales, sending a new burst of tingles everywhere. My hands close into fists, shocked that he's between my thighs right now.

His palms slide up from my calves to my thighs, then to the apex, pushing my legs to spread wider for him. In the next blink, his mouth is on my clit, sucking something fierce. He moves back and forth, licking up my soaked pussy juices to sucking my clit. He toys with my opening with the tip of his finger. It's enough to tease me and drive me a little insane, all in the same breath from wanting to feel him back inside my heat.

"You smell and taste so fucking good, Savannah. I wanna eat your pussy for breakfast, lunch, and dinner, baby."

"Y-you must be awfully hungry," I squeak out and then follow up with a wanton moan. This guy is passionate and seriously knows what he's doing in the hoo-ha department.

"You got such a pretty pink pussy…fuck," Sebastian rumbles and dives in. His scruff scratches my flesh lightly enough that I know my thighs will be burning if I pull on some jean shorts or pants anytime soon. I guess dresses it is for the rest of the week, but I have a suspicion that there will be a repeat if I wear them again. Not that I mind. If he wants to lick my pussy several times a day, I definitely won't be stopping him.

His thumb breaches my entrance while his drenched middle finger stretches the length to reach my ass. He toys with the back entrance, making my eyes roll heavenward, and a second orgasm consumes me. There's no holding it back this time as it hits full force. I noisily moan his name as I come. Anyone outside will hear me without an issue, but I can't help it, nor am I trying to. His touch feels far too great, and I don't want him to stop. The guys around here are bad boys—surely, they can handle some moaning and not lose any sleep because of it.

I breathlessly pant, "How did you go from our first kiss, to fingering me, to eating me out? And all in a span of maybe ten minutes?"

He chuckles, moving out from under my skirt after he slides my lace panties back into the right spot. Bash flashes a pleased smile. "I'd have my cock inside you right about now as well if you hadn't told me no already. Some may think it's all right to push further after snacking on a juicy peach, but I can respect your *no*." He winks, and it only makes me turn redder. I say redder, because I know I must be the color of a freaking tomato after all that.

My juices coat his lips, and it's incredibly erotic to watch him lick them, then groan with delight at my flavor. "I mean it, Angel, you have the tastiest, wettest pussy. Reminds me of eating a succulent, ripe piece of pineapple. *Fucking delicious*." His pitch ends on a growl, making me shiver with the need for his touch.

"You have to stop talking like that," I hiss. "Too much, Bash, too much!"

His brow crinkles as he places his hand on my hip. He squeezes, and I draw in a heavy breath. "Why's that? It's the truth."

I confess, "Because I won't be able to hold myself off for very long."

His expression brightens and he beams. "Challenge accepted." He chuckles and I laugh with him, shaking my head. "That's what I wanted—right there, baby. That smile will make a man move mountains for ya."

My mouth softens at his words. He went from sweet to sexy, to crude, and right back to sweet again. This man is truly going to be my end if I'm not careful. It'd be too easy and convenient to give in to his charm and let him take me for that wild ride. However, I want to live. If I'm not cautious, if I trust too quickly, then I may die. That's not a risk I'm willing to take…yet.

Chapter 6

The trouble is, you think you have time.

- Buddha

Bash

I ate her out…I licked that gushing sweet pussy of hers like a man starved, and for her, I was. She tasted like a mix between a ripe pineapple and a peach—my two favorites. How fitting it'd be her flavor. That was two days ago, and I still haven't stopped licking my lips and reminiscing. I've been walking around with a nonstop chubby, and my stomach's killing me from the absurd case of blue balls I've had. You know how hard it is to ride with a chubby and blue balls? Each bump is a blessing and a curse.

It's taken everything in me not to mention it to Savannah, but I promised myself I wouldn't pressure her. That's done nothing but result in me being a fucking prick to the brothers. Oh sure, they're highly entertained. They think this shit is hilarious, while I want to strangle my cock until the bastard eventually deflates.

Chaos shoots one of his signature glares in my direction. I'm used to his moodiness, so I take it in stride. "You need to get a handle on your shit."

I snort, rolling my eyes. He's one to talk, all wrapped up in his bitch. Not that I can blame him. I'm beginning to see the allure of having a woman around on the regular. Savannah has basically taken over any free time I have that I don't wrap up in the club, and it's not something I want to stop or slow down on any time soon.

"You're pissing the brothers off," he continues, not giving me a chance to respond. "Jinx and I may put up with your bullshit, but Sly or North will end up decking your ass if you bite their fucking heads off again. You're acting like a chick on her cycle. Either fuck your woman or else find a club whore to take care of it for you. Hell, they're all more than willing to take you up on any crumbs you'll offer in their direction. I swear those females are even more hooked on your ass since you wrecked your bike and roughed up your face." He shakes his head in disbelief.

I shrug, not surprised with them finding me more attractive like this. "Chicks always think they have a chance at fixing me, brother. Bitches haven't the slightest fucking clue about what goes on up here." I point to my head. "Nor do I want them to. If they saw some of the shit we've seen, they'd lose it." That's no lie either, Chaos and I have been through our fair share, cleaning up after his father's mess. Hell, I feel for the brother. There's no telling what he went through before we grew close, and I started prospecting for the club.

He concurs with a long sigh. "I feel you, brother. However, you're my VP. I can't have you all twisted up and shit over a woman or whatever it is. I'm just assuming it's an issue of the female variety since those types have the power to make us a touch fuckin' crazy."

I shoot him an intense look, stiffening up. "You know I always have your back, Chaos. If something is going down, you say the word, and I'll handle whatever you need me to. My loyalty won't stop, no matter what bitch I'm chasing after. You have my word."

He grunts, taking a hefty swig from the bottle of Fireball he's got sitting on the office desk. "Fuck. It seems like no matter what loose ends I tie up from my father, I discover something else the motherfucker was into."

"He was a sick, twisted fuck," I mutter, telling him the same thing I've said for years. His father's the whole reason I came into his club in the first place. Sure, I was destined for club life, but it was Chaos coming to me, that had me pledging my life and loyalty to the Kings of Carnage. The brother is my best friend; ain't no fuckin' way was I going to sit back while he dealt with his father's shit. He needed someone he could trust, and I vowed to always be that person. I may've joined under his father's rule, but my allegiance was to Chaos. In my view, he was always the true King in the club—nobody else.

"I'm sending North and the prospect to check it out. If anything is as bad as it sounds, we may need to roll out to handle it."

"You want me to hit up the brothers for church so we can discuss details?"

He shakes his head. "Not yet. If the intel turns out to be true, then we'll pop over to our field and come up with a plan. I don't know why, but I think the best when we're in the open, surrounded by nothing."

"I know how you roll, man. Just let me know when you're ready."

"Good. Until then, business as usual."

"Got it," I concede, heeding his orders.

The field he's mentioning is where we had our first meetup together, or what we refer to as our first official church session to discuss the takeover. Chaos had brought a couple of us in, told us what was going on with his father and asked us to help him clean house. Damn near every member from the original crew had to be taken out, along with his father. Back then, his dad was the active prez and Chaos was the club's enforcer. Our MC is completely different now. My brother has surrounded himself with a few close people he can trust. Not only that, but he's managed to get the club away from some really fucked up shit. We may deal drugs and guns, run protection, and various other adventurous jobs, but we don't beat, rape, and sell women.

He chin-lifts, and I look to where he's gestured. One of the club whores is making her way toward me. The bitch looks like she's on the prowl.

"Don't want any gash," I hiss out the side of my mouth.

He snickers. "Get your cocked sucked. You'll feel better."

With a grumble, I consider his words. The whore's not nearly as sexy as Savannah, but she's not bad. Maybe getting head would unwind my mind a bit…my little angel made it clear yesterday she won't be letting me fuck her anytime soon.

For a while, I'd even considered pursuing Chaos's sister. She's fairly young, but she's fucking gorgeous. She's been through enough shit with her father, and in the end, I figured she may have some deep-seated daddy issues. Me being much older than her might fuck her up even more. Not to mention it would piss my brother off, me looking at his younger sister like that. I eventually let the idea rest. I know I'd have enjoyed every minute of sliding into that cunt, and she'd have known what to expect with a member warming her bed.

Savannah has no idea about the lifestyle we live. She's green, and I swear that detail draws me to her even more. Truthfully, I'm not sure she could handle it if I were completely honest with her. Not that I think we'd go that far, but if we did…hell, even this trampy club whore knows more about the fucked-up shit I do than Savannah.

"Heya, Bash, you want some company?" she offers, folding her arms together, so her tits nearly pop out of the push-up bra she's got on. I look her over, taking in her bra and thong. She's not attempting to hide anything.

"You own a sundress?" I ask after a beat.

Her hand moves to flip her long dark hair behind her shoulder, then she reaches over to rub my bicep. I've got a navy T-shirt on under my vest, showing off part of the ink on my arms. "I have a minidress and a miniskirt." She blinks really fast. I wonder if she's attempting to bat her eyelashes at me or some shit. She doesn't need to try all that extra stuff. Men are easy to please. For one thing, we're visual creatures, and she's got her assets on display, so she's already got it covered.

"Nah, not the same thing."

She pops her bottom lip out into a pout, and I chuckle. That flirty pouting doesn't work on me. Maybe if my angel did it, then I'd take notice and want to do something about it. "I could ask around," she offers, and I shake my head.

"Don't worry about it. You don't need clothes on to suck my cock, anyhow."

"You want me right here?" She glances around, taking in everyone else. The prez is watching this exchange, no doubt amused by my requests. Every brother in here knows I have a thing for sundresses ever since my sweet Southern belle showed up in one, and I had it flying when we went for a spin. I'll never forget her surprised scream or melodic giggle when I took off. Damn, she felt good holding on to me like her life depended on it.

"Fuck it," I grumble, giving in to the temptation, hoping it'll clear my head a bit. "Why the fuck not."

She eagerly falls to her knees before me. Cookie likes to put on a show, striving to get whatever attention she can muster up from us grouchy bastards. We're at the strip club with North a lot, so the couple of club whores who hang around here get a little envious and try to amp their performances when the time strikes. They assume we're fucking the strippers twenty-four-seven rather than our easy club gash. I'm sure a few of us are dipping into the strippers' cunts, but I know the prez isn't, and neither am I. Cookie reaches for my belt buckle, yanking the metal and leather out of her way.

I stand still, watching her without making a move to offer any help. If she wants my cock bad enough, she's gotta do the work to have it. The bitch is lucky I'm willing to let her suck me off since her used up pussy has been around the club for so long. At this point, her ass should move to cooking and cleaning the rooms, yet she's set on having our cocks whenever we give them up. It's all good as long as someone still fucks her because no one stays here for free without giving us something in return.

Reaching over, I swipe Chaos's Fireball and take a hefty swig. The cinnamon-flavored liquor burns down my throat and into my chest. It's potent enough to warm me from the inside out and make my cheeks flush. The shit is fucking nasty. I don't know how the prez can drink it without a second thought. I'd rather sip vodka all night long and have a hefty fucking hangover the next day than drink Fireball. However, with Cookie below me and not Savannah, I need something to dull my senses a bit. I've only had one beer, not wanting to drink before I pick up my angel from work. At this rate, I'll have to borrow a truck. There's no way I'll carry my woman around on my bike when I've had more than one drink.

Every brothers' eyes are glued in our direction. No doubt in my mind it's because I've pushed club whores off me in favor of Savannah. My prez is right, though. I'm strung tight and could use a release. It's for the good of my club. I can't be all twisted up in my thoughts when there's business to take care of. I'm the VP. I don't have much room for fucking off on important shit. It's not like I'm committed to Savannah; we're not in a relationship. Yet, I've been holding off from free pussy. Maybe that was my mistake, and I shouldn't have held myself back.

Cookie flicks my jeans button free, and I take another swig of the liquor. Next, she lowers my zipper, and right then, the club door swings open. The door catches a gust of wind, flying all the way open to allow a burst of outside air in. The warmth hits me along with the bright light. It's been windy all day today. Always is this time of year.

I flick my gaze over, not too concerned. It's not like I can see much anyhow, being momentarily blinded by the blast of sunlight. Any asshole coming into the club who doesn't belong will be taken out by our enforcer. North's good about watching out for the clubhouse, as well as each of us.

Cookie's hands reach for my boxer briefs, and her fingertips graze my abdomen. My muscles tighten in response as my body readies itself for her to touch me lower. I glance back up, right as a petite woman comes barreling toward me. I meet the heated gaze of none other than the object of my desire, my latest fixation. Her irises blaze as she takes me in, slamming a to-go bag next to me on the bar.

"Angel," I breathe her nickname as my unspoken request has finally been answered. I've wanted to see her and kiss her all day. My hands jolt to Cookie's fingers to stop her from going any further. My stare remains pinned on my woman as I say, "I wasn't expecting you. I was going to come pick you up."

Her head bobs, and she releases a disappointed sigh. She flicks her gaze between me, Cookie, and the others around us. "I got off early. Thought I'd get an Uber to surprise you and bring you some dinner."

I glance at the white plastic bag beside me, then back to Savannah, realizing that it's for me. I swallow, feeling like an even bigger dick for wanting my cock sucked when this bitch was trying to do something nice and thoughtful for me. To show me that I was on her mind as well. I'm a goddamn dog who doesn't deserve her. "That's real sweet of you."

I look below to the woman still on her knees, waiting for whatever I tell her to do. I chin-lift, gesturing for her to get out of my way. "Not tonight," I tell her with a moody, unsatisfied growl. No matter how much my cock aches, I won't be getting sucked off when Savannah's around. The bitch has me far too intrigued for that shit. I won't disrespect her in front of my brothers, either. This is bad enough for her, I'm sure.

Savannah's quick as lightning as she moves to stand behind Cookie, resting her grip on the other woman's shoulders. "Oh, no," she argues, tauntingly. "You stay right there."

Cookie's shocked stare meets mine. She wants to obey me, as she should. It's the way the club works, but the fiery Southern belle behind her is demanding different. I'm a little lost as to what Savannah's up to, so I ignore the whore. "V-VP?" Cookie stutters out.

"The fuck is this, *baby?*" I question Savannah with a scowl. I can't handle a scene in front of the members. I'm already catching a ton of shit as it is, and I need their respect with my position. It's imperative. If they don't have respect for me, then they won't give a fuck when I tell them to take care of important business. It could be the difference between life and death.

"I don't want to interrupt." My woman glares right back and leans down to stage whisper loudly into Cookie's ear. "You were about to give him head; don't let me stop you. Take his pants off," she hisses. "Let's see what you're working with if it's even worth the trouble."

I nod at Cookie, telling her to listen. These bitches are off their rocker if they think I'll back down from this shit. If anything, it's sexy as fuck witnessing Savannah boss the club whore around, not to mention her little challenge about my size. "Do what she says."

I hear Chaos's grunt of amusement beside me, but I ignore him. I tune out everyone else but the two women before me, but I'm barely paying any attention to Cookie. The only reason she's anywhere near my thoughts is cause she's that close to my cock, and I don't want my dick hitting anyone's teeth.

The club whore sinks her fingers under the elastic of my underwear and tugs the front of them down enough for my cock and nuts to hang completely out and on display. I've fucked plenty of women around my brothers, so my cock isn't anything they haven't seen before. Savannah's gaze is challenging. She doesn't realize that sharing doesn't bother me…as long as it's not *her* I'm sharing. I lean forward until my lips are close enough to hers to graze and rasp, "It won't suck itself, Angel."

She inhales a quick, shaky breath. She may've done it quietly, but I'm close enough to catch it. I discovered when I was eating her pussy that she loves my dirty talk and for me to tell her what the hell to do. She's stubborn and headstrong, but she knows how to listen to me when she wants to come, or when she wants to feel me touch her somewhere. Her hold on the whore tightens, and she orders, "Grab his cock and start sucking."

I can't believe she's continuing to push this. I'm floored and turned on all at once. I didn't take her as a voyeur with the way she was worried someone would see us the other day when we were outside and I had my face buried between her thighs. "It'll do," I rasp, "But, I'd prefer *you* on your knees before me right now," I admit, flicking my gaze momentarily to Cookie. She's licking my cock like a fucking lollipop and bobbing on the head. She's a good little whore, but she's definitely not the bitch I want. "How's this work? You gonna take turns to finally get me off?"

Savannah's eyes pinch to slits, the challenge motivating her to be a bit more reckless. I like witnessing her like this…my little firecracker of a Southern belle is determined to prove herself at me by throwing down the gauntlet. Her hands go to Cookie's hair, and she wraps her fingers in the bitch's locks, holding tightly. Then, to my surprise, she shoves the gash's head forward. "Deep throat your VP," Savannah snips out the order loud enough for everyone to hear. "Apparently, you aren't getting him off."

Cookie chokes on my cock at first then relaxes her throat. She takes me in much deeper, the sensation feeling so damn good that chills prick over my flesh and my toes curl in my boots. The sight before me is like no other. Savannah controls the pace and the depth, and fuck my life, the bitch is hotter than fuck when she thinks she's in charge. Her chest heaves, panting as she watches the entire thing.

"Better," I growl, leaning in to kiss her.

Her head pulls back as she keeps my stare, denying me her mouth.

"The fuck?"

"You won't touch me while another chick has your dick in her mouth. I'll let you come, and I'll even watch, but you *won't* touch me."

Her little tantrum throws me over the edge, and my come jets into Cookie's mouth with so much force it'd knock me down if I weren't propped up against the bar. "Goddamn!" I roar as Cookie swallows me down, slurping away every last drop.

Cookie licks the head, cleaning me up before she's finished. She wipes her face, climbing to her feet, looking pleased with herself. "H-how was it, Bash?

I growl in her direction, then bark, "You don't even exist to me. I came for that bitch." I tilt my head, gesturing to my angel and watch as Cookie's eyes fill with tears. I'm a dick, but I don't really give a fuck right now—or ever. I'd warned the club whores many times before to leave me the hell alone unless I tell them differently.

Sapphire Knight

This eager bitch may've cost me the one thing I've wanted in a long ass time, Savannah Mae Lexington. If that's the case, Cookie will be lucky to make it until morning without me slitting her throat and tossing her out back to rot.

Sly grabs for Cookie, yanking her away from me. The brother can see I'm fuming inside, and when that happens, Bash comes out to play. I won't hit a woman, but you may get hurt being too damn close to me when I finally blow up and start punching shit.

Savannah steps into Cookie's spot before me, her hands going to my jeans. She yanks them up roughly, jostling my body with her own angry, jerky movements. "Put your dick in your pants," she snarls, and my chest reverberates in warning.

"Darlin'," Chaos thunders, his tone cautioning that she needs to watch herself.

I put my cock away, pushing closer until my nose is lined up with hers. "Want seconds?" I offer heatedly, and her hands land on my chest, shoving me away. My back slams against the bar.

"Fuck. You." Turning toward Jinx, she asks, "Will you please take me home?"

He bobs his head, heading for the door without a word.

"Don't you go anywhere!" I bellow as she turns heel. The bitch rolls her eyes with a huff and heads for the door, ignoring me. Her hand reaches for the handle, and I roar, "Don't you get on another man's fucking bike! I'll collect in blood!"

Her gaze scorches as she momentarily meets mine. "Fuck you, Bash," she rebukes and is outside in the next blink.

I shout, spinning around to slam my fists down onto the bar. "Motherfucker!" I punch the hard top again. The pain spiraling through my arms instantly sobers me up. I blink, taking in my surroundings as the feeling of disappointment eclipses my heart. I think I just fucked up and pushed away the one thing I want most.

My stony stare lands on the prez. I'm lost.

He cocks an eyebrow. "You gonna fucking cry about it, or you gonna go fix it?"

I bite the inside of my cheek, grabbing for his Fireball again. I chug the nasty shit and swipe the bag of food off the bar. I storm off, calling behind me, "Be back. Gonna have dinner with my bitch."

I hear a couple brothers laugh behind me, but ignore them.

"Don't you fuckin' hit Jinx!" Prez shouts in my wake.

I toss him the bird and make no promises. Jinx is a big motherfucker and my brother, but he should know better than to allow my bitch to get on the back of his bike. Savannah is mine. Sure, I'd told the brothers to back off her, but it just registered that she's really *mine*. I won't fuck this up and allow some other asshole to swoop in and play Captain Save a Ho.

I ride as if my ass is on fire, breaking my rule of not getting on my bike while drinking. Hell, I'm practically on fire with how irritated I am. I turn into the complex, my motorcycle roaring to a stop in front of Savannah's door. My brother's bike is already gone, and that's a good thing. Had he been here, I may've lost my temper, and I don't want to take our shit out on a brother. Not only that, but Jinx and I are usually close. I don't know what the fuck he was thinking, giving her a ride home, but we can discuss that shit once I've calmed down.

Storming over to the blue door, I pound my fist against it and yell, "Open the fuck up! I know you're in there." Several people will be peeping out their windows right about now. The nosey assholes always look out front when my bike pulls in, and now I'm out here screaming at my woman as well. I'm sure the neighbors are highly entertained. I don't give a shit about it either, as long as they don't attempt to call the law and report me.

"Go away, Bash!" she stubbornly yells back. She's close, I'd bet money her saucy ass is sitting right up against the door waiting for me.

"You know my full name, and it's not gonna happen. Open the fuck up, babe."

"Go back to your club and the other woman. I won't be bowing down to you any time soon!"

"Don't want any other women; you know that shit as well as I do. I want your pussy. This jealous tantrum wouldn't have happened if you'd let me inside you already."

"Oh, screw off. Don't you blame this on me, asshole."

"Let me in. We can talk about this inside the apartment. The nosey fucking neighbors are listening to us," I state lower, staring down the fuck stick next door. He catches my glower, and his blinds flick back in place, hiding his face. I can still see his shadow, though. Stupid nosey asshat.

"I don't care. Just leave."

"Damn it, woman. Don't make me break down this ugly door, 'cause I'll do it."

"And the cops will come. You'll go to jail," she replies tenaciously. I swear she mumbles something else, but it's too low for me to hear. She's all fiery right now, and I want to be all over her when she's like this.

"The hell I will, babe. Call 'em. See what they do," I remark cockily. "I'm not leaving until you let me in, and we talk through this issue." Or fuck it out of the way…but I leave that suggestion to myself for now.

She huffs, "Fine, but we're only talking for a minute, then you're leaving."

"Sure," I reply, without an ounce of truth. I'm not leaving until I smooth things over, and we're back on track again. We were making progress, but that got all sorts of twisted up today. I have to fix this without sticking my foot in my mouth, and there's a good possibility that'll be harder than I anticipated. One thing's for certain, I've never craved a woman as badly as I do Savannah. I'll do whatever it takes to make her mine.

Bash

Chapter 7

You've always had the power my dear, you just had to learn it for yourself.

- The Wizard of Oz

Savannah

I slowly open the door and stick my head out to find my asshole biker watching the door, waiting for me to let him inside. "You're infuriating," I breathe. "Leave me alone."

His stubborn sapphire stare meets mine, then he's pushing inside my apartment. He doesn't give me a chance to utter another word of protest as he slams the door closed again and shoves me up against it, his mouth smashing to mine. My palms flatten against his chest, moving to shove him like I did back at the club, but this time he's expecting it. His body is solid as I push, and he doesn't budge an inch. It's frustrating, and that irritation spills over into our lip lock. He kisses me fiercely, and I respond in kind, my mouth showing him how angry I am with the sharp bites I make to his lips. It does nothing to dissuade him. He only rumbles with pleasure.

Sebastian's hands move to my thighs, lifting me up higher for his sinful assault on my senses. My legs wrap around his hips as if they've done this a thousand times. His hard length is right there, teasing my clit as he applies pressure against my sex. I thought he felt big before and after witnessing him getting his dick sucked, I know he's above average in that department. My hips thrust forward, needing the friction, begging for more. My hands and mouth fight him. I don't want to make this easy for him, not after I helped that slut bring him pleasure. I've wanted him for weeks now and have refrained, doing the right thing. I'm sick of it.

I manage to break away, hissing, "Fuck you."

He leans in, biting my shoulder, sending enough chills over my body to make my nipples pebble. I've got on my clothes, including a bra, yet you'd think I was naked with the way my body responds to him. He hums and rasps, "I want to, so goddamn bad. You're driving me fucking crazy inside. You can hate me all you want for getting my cock sucked, but I had to, so I wouldn't force you into something you aren't ready for. I'm being patient for you. Don't you punish me for trying to be a better man for ya."

I let loose a humorless laugh, sarcasm lacing my voice. "Oh, so in other words, you were doing *me* the favor. How *thoughtful* of you for getting head all in the name of *me*. Prick."

His stormy irises meet mine. His nostrils flare as his own anger and desire churn inside him. "You think you could've handled me tonight? You get off work, kiss me and get me all worked up. Maybe I can't hold back like I did before and just eat your sweet pink pussy. Maybe this time, I rip all your fucking clothes off and decide to fuck that perfect little asshole of yours. You telling me you could handle it, the hard pounding I'd give you? You would take it like a good bitch and not fight me off? Cause the way you twist me up inside, you wouldn't be able to fight me. I'd be inside you before you could so much as scream *no*."

I slam my palms against him again. I'm left panting at his threatening promise. As he'd told me what would happen, I'd gone along and pictured it in my head, following his descriptions. Now I'm ridiculously turned on, my panties soaked with pent up desire. He paints a pretty sinful picture, one I've never experienced before. I was too busy living the good girl life before things went south, and I was forced to hide out. Now, I don't want any part of that old me...but rather, the way Sebastian views me. That's the person I should be, the one he explained in his fantasy. I need to be the sexy woman he can't keep his hands off of.

I meet his stony stare, fire blazing in my own, and I bite hard enough down on my cheek, it makes me want to yelp. Exhaling, I gather my emotions and thoughts to say, "What if you ripped my clothes off, and I didn't tell you no?" I continue, asking, "What if I begged you to put your dick inside me and fuck me relentlessly? How would you respond to that? Could you actually do it?"

He lets loose a deep sexual roar filled with desire, grabbing for the V-neck opening of my shirt. In the next beat, he's ripping it completely open, exposing my lacy fuchsia bra. "You gonna tell me no, Angel?" he mocks, his eyes daring me to try and fight after I'd practically egged him on to do it. "Tell me no this time. See if I fucking stop."

"Not yet," I breathe. "Keep going." My cheeks heat as I wait for Sebastian to continue. I knew I wanted him from the moment I saw him. I've tried to keep my distance from him—or any man, for that matter—to be patient and careful, but it's no use. He has my body strung so tightly right now, I feel as if I could combust just having him this close. I got a sample of what he's all about when he went down on me, and it's only forced my desire to multiply for him, making me feel needy and wanton.

"Fuckin' lucky you aren't in a dress today. I'd have bent you over and stuck my cock inside you already." He yanks my bra down underneath my breasts, freeing them. He stares at them for a beat before pinching the hardened crests. My core spasms with the zing of violent delight.

"Oh, God," I sigh with excitement. His hands are magic on my body. Sure, I've been touched before, but for some reason, when Sebastian does it, he lights me on fire. My body comes alive for him like no other.

The biker smirks then leans in and sucks one nipple in between his lips. I watch him, enthralled with his mouth on me again—this time in another place bringing me pleasure. He pulls away, switching to my other exposed breast. The sensation intensifies, and my head falls back against the door, my eyes slamming closed as I quietly moan to myself. It lasts moments before my breasts suddenly cold, missing the heat from his mouth.

He orders, "You watch me when I'm touching, licking, and fucking you, Sweet Pea. I want your eyes on me, always."

My lids part as I pick my head up and meet his stern gaze. He's so damn bossy, and rather than pissing me off, it makes me wetter for him. "What are you going to do if I don't follow directions very well? If I disobey?"

He chuckles. "I'll spank that ass before I fuck it, is what I'll do. You want me to redden your gorgeous booty, just say the word, baby." His lips lift into a confident grin, and then he's tossing me over his shoulder.

A shocked scream escapes me as Bash throws me off-kilter once again. He's constantly challenging me and surprising me with his actions and the things he says. I love it that he keeps me on my toes, never knowing what he's going to do next. I'm expecting him to take me down the hallway to my room and bed, but he doesn't bother. He walks straight for my tiny galley style kitchen, carefully laying me across my old farmhouse table. It's too big for the small space but when I saw it out by the dumpsters, I had to have it. I dragged it into my apartment, scrubbed it down and painted it white, and now it's my favorite piece of furniture. Someone's junk became my treasure. On the upside, it's sturdy enough to hold my weight without collapsing underneath us. It could probably hold four of me if I tried.

"You're crazy," I murmur, and he pauses long enough to flash me a wide smile.

"You're just now figuring that out? Baby, crazy could be my middle name."

"Well, that's reassuring."

His eyes turn serious. "I won't ever pretend to be something I'm not around you. You deserve real, and so do I."

I swallow, feeling his words in my soul. He's completely right, and all I've done is keep myself hidden from everyone, including him. He doesn't know why I'm really here or what I'm hiding. I wish I could tell him, but I can't bring myself to, no matter how much he's gotten under my skin. "I don't want you to pretend."

My words light the spark back in him, and he moves to yank my work pants off. I tilt my hips from side to side, giving him access. He tosses my shoes behind him into my living room and tugs my pants off the rest of the way. I lean up, twisting my torso a bit so my shirt can fall off. I leave my bra where it is. If Sebastian wants it off, I have no doubt he'll remove it. Besides, this way, the cups push my boobs up to give me even more cleavage.

"Christ. I knew you were an angel from the moment I saw you…but now, I think I've reached Heaven, Baby. You're so goddamn beautiful…you got me all sorts of tied up inside."

I bite my cheek, then allow a bright smile to break free. The irritation from earlier has disappeared as I take in the way he gazes down at my naked body, sprawled before him on my kitchen table. He worships me with his stare, and I've never felt so desired and accepted by another man. "Can I see you?" I whisper. The moment seems far too perfect to speak any louder—like I'll ruin it if I do.

He nods, and I bite down on my bottom lip, eagerly watching. He removes his vest, hanging it over one of the chairs. He reaches behind him, tugging his shirt off at the back of his neck, in the weird way men often do. His torso comes into view, and I swear I'll stutter if I have to say anything at the moment. He's chiseled, but also still bruised up something fierce from his wreck. My poor, injured biker. You'd never know it because he acts like it doesn't bother him in the slightest. If I wasn't around him so much, I'd miss his occasional winces and grunts of pain. I won't pressure him to lift me or anything again, the last thing I want to do is cause him more physical harm.

I was right about him being on the leaner side, but that's because he doesn't have an ounce of fat on him. The man has just the right amount of muscle on his frame to be strong but not bulky. He has my mouth watering as I think about trailing my tongue over every inch of his physique.

He smirks, never peeling his eyes away from me. He toes off his chunky big black biker boots and then shoves his faded jeans down. His cock springs free, and my legs automatically part. My pussy's on full display, offering my core to him. It happens without me thinking of doing it, like a natural reaction to seeing his hard cock so thick and close by. "So sexy and enticing, Savannah," he mutters, eyes glued to my open pussy. I'm so soaked for his touch that when the cool air hits me, I shiver with a chill. I need him filling me deep, warming me up from the inside like he did when he had me locked up against the front door.

His hand moves to squeeze his cock, and he pumps it while staring me down. I copy his regard, eagerly watching him jack his dick as I finger my pussy. I want to touch his length, to feel it stretching me open and take pleasure from him. "Please?" I sweetly beg, and his chest rumbles with satisfaction. He's thoughtful and kind and incredibly alpha when he's turned on. Clearly, the soft plea was just what he needed from me.

"Fuck," he gasps as my finger becomes coated in my wetness. He pulls my hand away, sucking my juices from the digit. Once he's satisfied he's gotten every drop, he releases it and presses his nose to my clit as he inhales deeply. "I love your scent. Christ," he comments, then swipes his tongue through my cream. He explores the entire area, licking my slit from my ass up to my clit.

It feels ridiculously good. I can't stop the moan from leaving my mouth. "Yes, just like that, Bash."

He's off me in a heartbeat, standing to his full height, wearing a moody glower. He folds his arms across his chest as I sputter from the sudden loss of his mouth. "What'd you call me?"

It takes me a moment to clear my head enough to think of what I'd said. "I called you Bash."

He shakes his head. "You've been callin' me Sebastian lately. I like it."

"Oh," I exhale. "Okay, then I can call you that instead."

He nods, satisfied once more, and dives in to continue licking me. Between sucking and nibbling my core, he grumbles. "Want my woman callin' me by my name. Bash is for the MC. This is you and me. Being real, and I want you knowing Sebastian, not the other asshole."

I manage not to giggle, although I want to from listening to him gripe at my pussy. It's kinda cute he gets all pouty over it. One minute he's storming in here, demanding to get his way, then he's saying sweet things and getting his feelings hurt because I called him by his MC name. Men say we're the difficult ones….

He slurps my juices, pushing a finger deep into my center, and I cry out. My orgasm begins to build, makes me clench everything up in anticipation. He feels me tighten my core and thrusts faster. He learned yesterday that it makes me shoot off like a rocket. "Better come for me, baby. Give me what I want, when I want it," he orders, pushing another finger in deep and my body obeys, folding to his demands.

"Sebastian!" I cry in bliss, and he stays right with me, pumping as I ride out every last moment of my explosive orgasm.

"Mm, now I'm gonna feel that tight wet cunt wrapped around my cock." He leans over me, bringing his mouth to mine. We kiss. It's easy to get caught up in his kisses. His tongue is demanding, yet not overwhelmingly so. It's like meeting an old friend and sharing a warm embrace, only more. I could kiss him for hours and love every second of it.

I release a gasp of surprise as he suddenly thrusts his length inside me. He didn't need to line himself up or anything, one minute he was there, and the next, he was deeply seated in my core. My pussy burns a bit as he stretches me wider than my fingers usually do. I haven't been with a man in a while, and the last one was only average in dick size. Sebastian fills me, and the sensation is marvelous, exactly what I was craving from him.

"Fuck," he grunts. "This pussy has just been waiting for me to fill it, hasn't it, babe?"

"Yes! You feel really, really good," I murmur, ensconced in his warm embrace.

"You needed to be fucked, didn't you?" he asks. I draw his bottom lip into my mouth, sucking on it a moment before I release it to nip along his jaw. "I understand why you're feisty now. This pussy is what dreams are made of." He peppers kisses over the tops of my breasts, leaving little love bites and purple marks behind.

The wooden table's painfully hard, and as he increases his quick, punishing pace, he wraps an arm underneath me. It helps to act as a sort of barrier between my back and the wood, and I'm touched at his efforts to make sure I'm comfortable. It's not necessary, though, as the orgasm he gave me was plenty to relax my mind and muscles. He clenches me tightly to him, his hips making sharp jerky thrusts. It's so different than having his mouth and fingers working me over. It's more intimate, and his body heat warms my skin. I want to cling to him and never let go.

My core squeezes at the thought of keeping him near me for the long haul, and he groans. "Best pussy, Savannah. Not giving this cunt up. Gonna put anyone that thinks they can touch you six feet under. This is your warning, Sweet Pea. I don't share. I'll rain down hell on any motherfucker who thinks they can cross me on it too."

I pull his face to mine, my mouth taking his in a tense, blistering kiss. His words are everything I want to hear, even though I shouldn't. I can't afford to get wrapped up in a man like Sebastian, yet I can't seem to stop myself either. He doesn't deserve the complications I come with. I could put him in danger, and that's the last thing I'd want for him. No one deserves to die because of me.

Sebastian breaks my kiss, murmuring, "Gonna come, Angel. I need you there with me." He reaches between our bodies, seeking my clit. He rubs over it with his middle finger, making me scream out with the sudden onslaught of sensations. As if having his length inside me wasn't enough, now my body's on overload. "That's it, Savannah, give your man what he wants. Squeeze that tight cunt around my cock and milk me."

"Oh, my God!" I yell as bliss crashes through me, taking me under. His groin pistons, the intensity sure to do some damage and make me sore tomorrow. I feel overwhelmed, completely smitten with him, and there's no turning back at this point. I don't know if I'll be able to let him go if I need to in the future.

Hot liquid fills my core, shocking me as I realize he never slipped on a condom before entering me. How could I be so reckless? It's not like I can go to a doctor's office for a checkup or anything; that would chance bringing unwanted attention to me, and I can't have that.

"Y-you didn't wear a condom!" I sputter, attempting to catch my breath, still in shock.

He grunts, shaking his head into my shoulder. I should feel enraged, yet I can't bring myself to it. I like the way his cum feels inside me. He mutters against my neck, "Not wearing a condom with *my* woman."

"And how many women are yours, exactly? This is concerning; vagina health is important."

He pulls back, the rapture escaping his features as seriousness reflects back at me. "Just one. *You.* I don't fuck around and call women mine if I don't really mean it. You're the first for me, and that's why I wasn't wearing a condom with you. If I was gonna fuck other bitches, I'd wrap it up. I'd never hurt you like that."

"You got head from one of them, one of those not-your-other-women," I point out, being a smartass and not making much sense. It doesn't matter, though, because I understand what I'm saying, and luckily Bash is smart enough to get it as well.

"That's different."

I huff and roll my eyes, not about to buy into his bullshit at the moment. I attempt to move away, but he doesn't let me go anywhere. *Stubborn biker.*

"I was trying not to pressure you. I explained that to you when you showed up. We weren't exclusive, and I was only letting Cookie suck me off until I saw your face. Once you walked into the bar, I knew that bitch could never satisfy me, not as long as I have you in my life."

"Yet, you got off. I was there; I watched the entire thing!"

"'Cause you were there throwing a fucking tantrum, and it was sexy as fuck. Never had a bitch take control of another female while she was sucking my cock. You have no idea how erotic you were. *You*! No one else." He leans in, nudging my nose with his. "Don't start this shit, or else I'll go right back to fuckin' you. I won't give you a break either like I'd intended to."

I fight against it, but I'm not strong enough to fully hide my grin from his explanation. Hearing him rationalize it like that, saying I was the one calling the shots. It makes me feel as if I was in control, and that's exactly what I was striving for when I decided to make a point of it to him at the club. "Does this new label make you *mine*, as well, or is this situation supposed to be one-sided?"

He cocks an eyebrow, his blue irises sparkling. He's enjoying all of this far too much. "You gonna let me fill this pretty pink cunt up whenever I want to with my tongue, fingers, and cock?"

My eyes widen. "I'm sure we could work something out, depending on the circumstances."

He grins. "Like I said before, babe…don't want any other bitch." It's not a straight out yes or no, but I'll take it. He's a biker, used to being wild and free. I have a feeling it's going to take a little while for him to get used to the idea of our new labels, of me reeling him in, even if he's the one who started handing out the branding first. I should be happy he's not literally trying to stamp his name on me somewhere.

"I have one request if you plan on keeping up this pace."

His brow scrunches. "Did I hurt you too badly?"

I shake my head. "I loved it."

He visibly relaxes, pressing a quick kiss to my lips. "Then what is it, Angel?"

"Take me to my bed, Sebastian. It's my turn to show you how I move my hips." I wink, and he chuckles.

"You're gonna be the fucking death of me, Angel. The sweetest, fucking death," he says as he lifts me in his arms, careful to keep his hefty dick tucked firmly inside my heat. He carries me toward the hallway that leads to my bedroom, and I grin the entire time. We've got a lot of makeup sex to have, and I'm going to make damn sure he doesn't hesitate to say no the next time a woman offers him a blowjob.

Sebastian is mine. I claimed him, and those other club women better back off.

Sapphire Knight

Chapter 8

Vulnerability:

The last thing I want you to see in me. The first thing I look for in you.

- Brene Brown

Bash

My fingers trail through Savannah's silky hair as I watch her sleep soundly, her creamy flesh looking beautiful against her lilac sheets. How I ended up meeting someone like her is beyond me. I have to chalk it up to fate because without that wreck, I don't think I'd have found her anytime soon. She's way out of my league, and I'm taking advantage of having her while I can. I may be brash and rough around the edges at times, but I'm no idiot.

I've been solely focused on the club. After Chaos took over, it's been one day at a time rebuilding to where the MC needs to be. It's taken time and patience for each of us to establish good business connections and bring in a decent payday. After getting the KOC away from dealing in flesh, it hit another low. We were out of money and down to a skeleton crew. Chaos has been in the life for God knows how long, so he knew how to climb out of the hole.

It took all of us doing our share, but we made it. Now our days are filled with jobs, pussy, and club life. I bring in my fair share by dealing to Atlanta's elite drug users, as well as provide the locals with their hookup. Sly does his part by collecting protection money from some businesses as well as betting. North has his hands in deep with the strip club, and Jinx runs drugs through the railroad. It's right in his back yard—or damn near, anyhow—and he takes full advantage of the convenience.

Out of nowhere, this angel drops into my life and leaves my head spinning. I think I took one look at her and was a goner from that moment on, even if it was a few weeks until I realized that I have it bad and admitted it to myself. I'm a stubborn ass at times, and where Savannah is concerned, it seems to amplify tenfold.

"Sweet Pea," I rasp, leaning in to place soft kisses along her shoulder. She's on her belly, head facing the opposite way. I'd fucked her all night and worn her ass out. It's nearly noon now, and I've got shit to do. I know she has to work sometime today as well. Probably two p.m. or so—it's her usual shift.

"Mm?" she mumbles sleepily and stretches, kicking the sheet away from her gloriously naked body. She's breathtakingly beautiful, curvy in all the right places with a juicy ass. Seeing my cum dried between her thighs makes her even more enticing. She's fucking sexy.

I move my hand to her back, running my rough palm over her silky-smooth skin. If I didn't have to make a drop, I'd take her again right now. "I have to handle some shit…gonna take me out of town. What time do you work?"

She stays on her belly but turns her head to meet my sated gaze. "I go in at two. I have the dinner shift again."

I nod, bringing my hand up to smooth my knuckles along her jaw. "I'll be out of town for most of the day. You gonna be good?"

She smirks. "I may be walking a little funny; otherwise, I'll be okay."

A chuckle breaks free as I take in the ten or so hickeys I left during our various activities. I don't doubt it for a moment that she's feeling me everywhere. I did that shit on purpose. Everyone will see that I've made her mine.

She flashes me a quick look, mentioning, "You can go do whatever you need to. I'll call an Uber for a ride."

My grin drops, and I release a grumble of protest. "You never know what kind of twisted fuck is driving an Uber, babe. It's different if your ol' man is with you, but alone, I don't like it."

She rolls her eyes, turning her face back in the other direction. She's sassy and independent, two things that drive me mad for her, but also up the wall. I respect her, but I also want to make sure she's safe. I've lived the rough life for many years. I know what kind of assholes lie in wait to prey on pretty, perfect bitches like my Sav.

"Hey, don't shut me out. I'm being rational, not a dick."

She sits up, fully facing me. The sheets rest below us, and her tits are right there on display for me. The sight is entirely too enticing, begging for my touch. I'd be all over her in a heartbeat, but I have to go and make some serious cash for the club and to spoil her with. "My car is still broken, Sebastian. I don't want to Uber either and spend cash I need to save, but I don't want to ask anyone else for a ride either. Sly offered before, and it didn't feel right, even if he is a nice guy."

A possessive growl rumbles my chest. "No shit, it didn't feel right, 'cause it's not. You're *mine*, Angel. Don't forget that important detail."

"You've made yourself abundantly clear. I heard you say it last night. It's all good, as long as you remember it goes both ways, VP."

My face lights back up at her claim. She's just as stubborn as I am, and I like it. A lot. "I actually have a solution to this problem. I'm going to leave you my key fob, and you'll take my car. Unlike yours, mine won't leave you stranded, Sweet Pea."

Her mouth drops open. "You own a car? This entire time you've had me ride on your motorcycle and haven't once bothered to mention that you have a car? I've worn my hair in a braid for weeks because I thought there wasn't another option!"

With a snicker, I shake my head. "There isn't another option. If I didn't have to jet, then you'd be on my bike today too. Since that's not the case and I don't want you with anyone else, you can take my car to work. At least I'll have the peace of mind that you're safe and not gonna break down anywhere or get kidnapped by some random psycho. I'll have to see you tonight when I get back. All right?"

She concedes with a nod. "I can bring us some dinner."

"Sounds perfect, baby. I'm also leaving you with a burner phone. Can't have you without a way to reach me." I press a kiss to her forehead and lean over to her bedside table to assist me in getting out of bed. Last night was fun, but my ribs are screaming in protest today. Her bed must be a full-size or something, 'cause I was squished up to her all night. Not that I minded one bit or anything, busted ribs and all.

In fact, I'm going to make a call today and get a bigger bed delivered. I doubt she wants to be at my place all the time in our near future, or else I wouldn't bother. If I'm going to be spending time over here, which I plan to, then we need a bigger bed. I find my jeans and dig around in my pockets until I find what I need. I hand her the key fob along with the cheap disposable phone. "It's in the back, parked in front of my place."

She nods, offering me a sweet smile. "Okay. Thank you, Sebastian. You have no idea what this means to me, how much I appreciate you trusting me with these. What color is the car, so I don't look like an idiot wandering around back there?"

"It's the destroyer gray Charger. Powder-coated rims, black windows."

"Why am I not surprised you'd have a vehicle with paint called destroyer gray?" She laughs, and I shrug, not disturbed in the slightest by her cute attempt at ribbing me.

"If I'm gonna be stuck driving a car around, it won't be anything ugly. The thing just sits there anyhow; I prefer my bike. It should still have a full tank, so you don't have to worry about anything, just driving."

"Thank you, Sebastian. Really."

Wearing a smirk, I climb on the bed to lean over to press a kiss on her pouty lips. "I'm out. See you tonight, gorgeous," I say against her mouth and kiss her again because it's hard to get enough of her. Especially when she's so beautiful like this. She makes my heart beat overtime.

Savannah offers me a bright smile as I hop out of bed, snatch my jeans again, and head for the living room. I'd tossed my clothes off between there and the kitchen last night, so I have to hunt them down. I'd grabbed my jeans sometime in the middle of the night, in case the club hit me up for an emergency, but that was it. Once I get them yanked back on, ribs protesting and all, I hear the shower turn on. With one last glance around the place, I lock the door and close it behind me. I wish I could hang around here all day and continue exploring her delectable body, but that'll have to wait. If she's up for it tonight, though, I'll pick back up where we left off.

I straddle my bike and send off two texts. The first one is to a prospect, telling him to get his ass over here to watch out for Savannah. I can't remember the guy's name, but he's only a prospect, so it's not something for me to worry about. I don't want my woman to know I've got a guy on her, but I want him close enough in case she needs help for any reason. This area likes to cast their judgments on the MC and the life we choose to live. Their opinions may've been somewhat deserved in the past with the sex trafficking. Still, I don't want any of those convictions extended toward my woman. We live out here to be away from the masses, yet it makes us stand out to the locals since there aren't very many.

The second text goes out to my brother, Jinx. Aside from Chaos, Jinx would be the other brother I'd consider myself to be really close to. That's why I felt comfortable enough for us to make this deal together. I needed a partner based on the amount of blow this big-time buyer wants.

With how much he requested, I need to get cocaine by the goddamn truckload to fulfill this new asshole's order. That requires Jinx being part of the cut…not that I mind.

It's too much of a risk if I bring in that much powder alone. However, if we divide it up, and my brother's responsible for half, then it'll be less likely to raise any red flags. He can bring in a shit ton using his railroad system. At the same time, I can make up for anything else we need by my furniture delivery contact. I have a guy who moves my product inside his furniture orders, so the cops don't catch on.

I let Jinx know I'm headed toward the club so we can meet up and ride into Atlanta together. Most of the brothers don't mind the city, but personally, I can't stand it. There's always boatloads of traffic, and if it's a specific time, you're basically fucked if you're in a hurry to go anywhere. Not only that, but there's the gang presence as well. I already have to watch my back with my MC colors and skin tone pissing enough people off, but then you throw in some of those wannabe thugs, and all hell breaks loose. I've been randomly shot at more times than I can count, and the moment you shoot back, there's a news story on another young life being taken. They like to leave out the details about how he was a punk thug, shooting at bikers like he was some kind of badass motherfucker when he was really a fucking troublemaker trying to step foot on turf he doesn't run.

As you can tell, I'm jaded on that subject. I have little sympathy for fucknuts who go out stirring up trouble when there doesn't need to be any. I'm all about live and let live, as long as you stay the fuck outta my way.

The turnoff to our MC comes up, and I notice Jinx. He's straddling his idling bike at the end of the road where it meets the main road I'm on. He's waiting for me, I assume. I slow down, chin-lifting his way, and he hits the road, easily catching up to me as we head for the city.

Jinx is our road captain, so I fall behind him a foot or so. He can pick the route we'll take, and I'll follow. I'm familiar with the areas, but he's always got directions planned out the best way. I wouldn't ask him to take over my club shit, so I don't attempt to step on his toes where the road is concerned. Besides, it's a good feeling being able to let someone else that you can trust in, to handle their share. Less for me to worry about.

The ride goes by too quickly for my liking. I've always been a big fan of longer road trips. I had some much-warranted time with my thoughts—Savannah Mae being at the front and center. I love to ride and don't mind the business side of this life, but today I find myself wanting to be back in bed with her. Our fucking was straight out phenomenal, but I also enjoyed waking up next to her warm body and feminine flowery scent. I'd assumed that once I fucked her, it'd take away some of her allure over me, but I was mistaken. We'd gone back to her bedroom and she'd rode my cock until I saw stars. Each time after seemed to get even better. However, it's hard to believe that's possible considering the first time I was inside her was pretty goddamn epic.

"You ready for this?" Jinx asks once we've walked our bikes backward to park. We're tucked up close to a warehouse owned by our buyer. We've had prospects riding through here for the past week, watching over the area in case we were being set up. Each day their reports check out to be straight, so here we are.

I shrug, cutting my engine. I grab my smokes from my saddlebag, offering one to Jinx before lighting up. He takes me up on it. I don't smoke often, but when I have a decent-sized deal going down, my nerves call for the nicotine. It helps me remain calm, and in this business, that's imperative. If you're wigging out and not thinking straight, shit can head south quickly. "Not gonna lie and say that there isn't someplace else I'd rather be."

His brow wrinkles as he bobs his head. He questions, "Your woman that good?"

"Fuck, man. Good isn't a strong enough description for it. She has me all sorts of twisted up inside. When you took her home, I about lost my shit. Showed up pounding on her door until we worked through our issues. I decided I was over being patient, done waiting on her schedule."

"You thinking about claiming her?"

"Making her my ol' lady?"

He nods.

I exhale a cloud of smoke, my shoulders bouncing. "Crossed my mind around three a.m. when I was dumping deep inside her cunt for the fourth time."

He smirks, not replying as a luxury SUV pulls in beside us. A man gets out of the passenger side and opens the back door. Our client steps out, looking every bit the part of a successful billionaire. While making back-alley deals is beneath him, given the nature of this, I insisted I meet with him and no one else. I don't make agreements with middlemen—never have and damn sure won't start now.

Jinx and I both vacate the bikes, approaching our buyer. I toss my cigarette to the ground, smashing it out with my boot. "Maliki," I chin-lift to the prominent African American businessman and take note that none of his guys approach us, giving us privacy. He's a wolf in sheep's clothing. His brother was even worse before he was murdered, but I never had any dealings with him. I'd heard through the grapevine how he'd fucked over a variety of different people. I kept my distance, not wanting any part of what he was offering. Being a drug dealer is tough enough evading jail time, that I stay far the fuck away from people known to screw others over.

Maliki, however, is a different story. He makes many of his more lucrative business deals during his ostentatious parties. He's somewhat famous for them on the streets. Not that any of us common folk would ever get invited. We're not rich enough. We only know about them from his tall orders and overboard requests—the streets like to talk. He's the type of man that if he wants something, it doesn't matter how low he has to go, he'll achieve it. Some of his past dealers have bragged about doing business with him and they've wound up dead. I'm not a fucking idiot like they were, and neither is Jinx. When business goes down, we keep that shit to ourselves to ward off any potential heat or threats from coming our way. Not only that, but Jinx and I have each other's backs. Always.

"Bash," Maliki greets, flicking his shrewd gaze to my brother.

"This is my brother, Jinx. He's another officer in Kings of Carnage."

He nods to Jinx. "You're the other dealer Bash recommended to me, I take it."

Jinx agrees. He's not a man of many words; he's been that way the entire time I've known him. His big, Samoan ass doesn't like anyone except his brothers, my guess is it's because of the way he grew up back in Hawaii. If he doesn't know you, he won't say shit to you. It makes some people nervous, but I actually prefer it. I know he won't chitchat randomly about anything unless he means it or finds it necessary enough to notate.

Maliki exhales, turning to me. "I'm glad you're both in the same MC and officers with positions of power. I wasn't keen on splitting up this deal, but this doesn't bother me as much as it did when you'd previously brought it up."

"Jinx is straight. I trust him with my life. I'd never have put him up for the job if I believed differently."

He steeples his hands, flicking his attention between my brother and me. "Will we need to negotiate on the price, or do you honor Bash's deals, Jinx?" Maliki inquires, making my shoulders tighten. He should've asked me this over the phone. It's not cool to question things when we're already here to arrange transport and take a deposit. If he wasn't spending so much cash, a question like this could potentially have him lose everything. Hell, in the past, it'd have him losing his life as well.

Jinx flashes me an irritated glance, no doubt thinking the same thing I am. He eventually nods, knowing how much money we're going to be bringing in. "I'll help with the product. You pay Bash for it, and he'll give me my cut. Make it easier on everyone." He flicks his cigarette to the ground and stomps it out.

I release a tense breath, grateful for my brother going easy on this. He must realize how important this deal is to me. It could bring in more contacts in the future. Maliki is big in the drug world as far as buying is concerned. He orders enough that I could stop dealing to most of my smaller tweakers and only concentrate on supplying a few key players.

I'd be bringing in plenty of cash flow, and it'd significantly reduce my risk of being caught by the cops.

I send Jinx a grateful chin-lift, letting him know that I appreciate what he's done. He knows I'll square him up on his take and not fuck him over. We may hate everyone else, but in our club, loyalty is imperative.

I stretch my neck, moving it from right to left and tell Maliki, "We can have everything you requested by Friday. You pay half upfront like the last time we did business and half when it's delivered." I'd sold him a smaller amount in the past—a tester if you will. He liked what I had to offer and decided he wanted me to be his main supplier, based on the quality.

Maliki gestures to the man still standing beside the back-passenger door. We all watch as he rounds the vehicle, opening the hatch. He's behind the SUV for a moment before returning with two solid black backpacks. He hands one to me and the other to Jinx.

Maliki motions to the bags. "Just as you instructed. The bags are insulated and packed full of hundred-dollar bills." I always request the money in a nondescript black backpack. It's easier for me to ride with, and I don't have to worry about strapping it down. Believe it or not, but when money is stuffed in the right way, the bags can be fairly heavy. You think paper doesn't weigh anything, but stick a couple packs of printer paper in a bag and tell me the shit doesn't weigh anything.

"Sounds good. We'll put in our orders and get our end of things rolling in place. I take it we met here because this will be the drop-off point as well as the initial exchange?"

The billionaire agrees. "There will be two SUVs parked out here. The bay will be lifted when you arrive so my employees can download the product. You'll get the other half of your payment and be on your way. My help will make sure everything is reloaded and taken to my personal location. I won't be here when you arrive, and if for any reason you don't see the two SUVs I mentioned, keep driving and call me directly."

"We can handle that, no problem."

"It's been a pleasure." He tilts his head toward us. "I have to get back to my business, as I'm sure you do as well."

"Yeah." I agree, ready to get the fuck out of here. I'm sure my brother is as well. I don't like being in this area without having the rest of my brothers for backup in case shit goes south.

He turns away, then pauses suddenly. "Oh, one more thing," Maliki begins and reaches inside his suit jacket. He pulls a photo free from the inside pocket and says, "I've been looking for a friend's daughter. She's been gone a while, so there's no telling where she could be. Would you let me know if you come across anyone who resembles her? I'll pay handsomely for any information on her whereabouts."

"Oh, sure, what's her name?" I reach for the photo. I doubt I'll ever see whoever he's searching for, but I'm not going to tell him that outright and chance fucking up our deal in any way. Kings of Carnage don't deal in human flesh anymore, so the only women we pay any mind to is the club whores around the club who willingly want to be there.

"Savannah Lexington," he replies, gesturing to the photo in my hand that I hadn't looked at yet.

My free hand curls into a fist as I fight every muscle in my face to not show any sign of recognition at the name. My eyes flick to the image, and I swallow. My chest aching at the picture of my angel smiling back at me. Exhaling, I shake my head. "Nope, never seen her before. I'd remember her if so…damn." I move to hand the photo back, but he stops me, gesturing to Jinx.

"Maybe he's seen her?"

My eyes meet Jinx's, silently begging him not to give up Savannah. We've been around each other long enough that I think we can tell when one of us isn't feeling something. As much as it pains my chest to do so, I grit my teeth and hand him the image.

He stares down at it for a beat, and I know he's aware of who she is. There's no denying that's the same woman who's been on the back of my bike damn near every day since she showed up at the compound, and we had lunch together. I'm bracing myself for him to offer her up when he shakes his head. "It's no one I've ever fucked." He gives the photo back to Maliki and straddles his motorcycle without another word. I don't doubt it for a moment that he'll be bringing this up later. Can't say I blame him. I'd do the same if the roles were reversed.

Maliki moves to hand me the photo again. "Keep it. I have copies. If you see her, please reach out."

I tuck the image inside my cut. "Of course. We'll be back on Friday to finish up."

"Until then," he comments and heads back to his SUV. I watch as his man opens the back door and then closes it once Maliki is tucked inside. His guy meets my stony gaze before getting into the front passenger side, and they drive away.

"Later," I growl to Jinx before he can mention it. "I need to hear her out first." He doesn't respond, he just fires his motorcycle up. I swing my leg over my seat, starting my ride and follow once he takes off.

This is a goddamn cluster fuck. Savannah has a lot of explaining to do.

We head back to the club, and Jinx veers off before we leave Atlanta entirely. He's got his own shit to handle, and I trust him to keep this new information about Savannah between us. If I didn't trust the brother with my life, I wouldn't be working with him on a deal this large. It could put us away for many years if the wrong person caught wind of it.

I make it back to the compound to find Chaos outside, leaning against the old firehouse that serves as our club. Out of anyone in the MC, he needs to know what just happened. I open up and bring him up to speed on my deal with Jinx and how it has to do with Maliki. Chaos is familiar with the billionaire. His twisted dead brother was into the sex trade, amongst many other crooked ways to scam people out of their hard-earned money.

"Told me that his friend is searching for his daughter. He's got to be fucking lying. Savannah mentioned that her father is dead." I take a drag from my cigarette. The second one today due to one asshole.

He folds his arms across his chest, saying the one thing I don't want to hear. "Or else maybe she's lying to you, brother."

"Fuck off," I grumble, with an irritated exhale.

His hand clamps onto my shoulder, and I flick my gaze back to his. "Keep your eyes open. It's too easy to be blinded by a pair of tits. You need to hear this shit. That's why I'm sayin' it."

I nod, taking a long drag from the menthol. "I hear you. I also remember all of the bullshit Maliki's brother was in bed with your father over, and besides that, I believe Savannah. If you'd have seen how fucking tore up she was about her father being dead, you'd understand why I trust she's telling the truth."

"Whatever you decide to do, whether it be to offer her up to him, hide her away, or fight for her…I've got your back. The MC will have your back. Maybe Sly can find some more info on it all for you. He knew some big shots with the bets and fighting and whatnot."

"Appreciate that, man. I'll talk to him," I choke out, holding my knuckles out for a fist bump. I've always backed him on whatever he needed inside the club or out, and to have him pay me the same respect in return, it makes me feel some type of way. He's not just my MC brother; he's my brother by choice.

Chaos meets my knuckles as my Charger comes into view, the blacked-out windows effectively hiding the beautiful woman behind the wheel. I toss the rest of the cancerous cigarette to the ground, smashing it out with the toe of my boot. I don't want Savannah coming around me while I reek of cigarette smoke. She always smells all flowery or like burgers when she's around me, and I don't wanna stink to her.

"Hm," he hums, leaning back against the building.

My angel surprises me when she pulls my car into one of the lined spots, right next to my bike in the parking lot. It's nowhere near the time she's usually off. Having her here right now kind of sets me on edge after what happened with Maliki today. My heart speeds up, worried that she's here for a reason that I'm not going to like. I frown, waiting for her to get out and tell me what's going on.

Chaos emits a low whistle, uttering, "Damn, it's like that now, huh?"

I roll my eyes and grumble in response. Of course, I'm gonna catch shit for letting my woman drive my car. The brothers never see me driving the damn thing, let alone allowing a female to.

"Tell me you at least tapped that pussy."

"I've licked that cunt, fingered it, and fucked it. Filled it with my cum four times last night."

"*Fuck.* That good?" His brows lift with interest, already moving past the seriousness from moments before. If he were anybody else, I'd be getting possessive and shit, but he's my prez. I know he asks 'cause it's his place to be in the middle of all our business. Not only that, but the nosey asshole's my best fucking friend. We don't keep shit from each other…haven't for a long time.

I meet his stare, admitting, "Best I've ever had." He casts his regard to my woman, observing as she climbs out of the sleek car, happily beaming in my direction. "Glad she had the blacked-out windows and different ride, after learning what I did today."

Chaos nods, not mentioning anything else as Savannah approaches. "Hey, you," she says my way, before greeting my prez. "Hello, Chaos."

He chin-lifts at her before telling me, "We'll talk more on it later."

"Bet." I watch as he strides away and then face my angel. She makes me all warm and fuzzy inside. The feeling's foreign, and I don't really know what to do with it. I want to put the bitch in my pocket and keep her next to me all the damn time. "Hey, Sweet Pea. Wasn't expecting you yet. Everything okay?"

She grins, wrapping her arms around my middle to tuck in close. She peers up at me and divulges, "The diner was slow, so I got to leave early. Normally, I'd stay and close, but when they mentioned one of us getting off early, I asked first. I was hoping for a repeat of last night," she admits, licking her lips.

She's sexy as fuck, wanting my cock.

"Tonight was the chicken fried steak and mashed potato special, so I brought some for you."

And my bitch brought food, too. She's definitely a keeper.

Her thoughtfulness makes my lips tip into a smirk. I've been stressed the fuck out since Jinx, and I rode away from Maliki. Having her in my arms is finally giving me a moment to breathe easily again. "You're always thinking of me, yeah?" I put my nose to the top of her head, taking in the flowery smell from her shampoo. It's the scent I'd been thinking of all damn day after spending the night breathing it in from her pillows. I press a kiss to the silky locks, and reach up, tugging the elastic band out of her hair. She had it pulled into a tight ponytail for work, but I prefer it when it's wild, and I can wrap it around my fist.

She dips her chin, her cheeks turning pink. "You do sweet things for me, too, and you let me drive your car today without a second thought. The least I can do is make sure you have something to eat."

I squeeze her tightly. "Trust me, babe, I gave you driving my car around multiple thoughts today," I tease, making her grin.

She smacks my stomach, making me hiss from my bruised ribs. "Oh, hush, your car was perfectly fine with me driving. I didn't run anyone over or anything if that's what you were worried about. I even went the speed limit, though I can feel it has some power when I give it gas."

Gesturing to the car, I tell her, "Yeah, it does. Now get your sexy ass back in there, Angel. I'll follow you to the apartment. We can eat then. I'm diving between those thighs for some dessert. Plan to make you whimper my name again, just like last night."

"Yours or mine?" Savannah asks, and everything inside me screams at me to tell her it's gonna be *our* place and *our* stuff in it before she can blink and attempt to offer up a protest. I don't say jack, however, not wanting to frighten her off. I gotta let her get used to the idea of us being a thing before I start really laying down my plans of the future with her.

It's been a few weeks. I don't plan on losing her before I have my hooks in deep.

After being intimate with her all night and then watching her sleep, it caused me to think long and hard. I had time to realize exactly what I want in my future, and it has her front and center. *One thing's for sure, though. I've got to get her to tell me why in the fuck Maliki's hunting her.*

Bash

Chapter 9

Hard truth: You cannot change things by loving them harder.

- @liveinthedetails

Savannah

"Angel," Sebastian rasps, meeting my gaze as he strides through my apartment door. I parked his car in front of my place so he'd know I was here waiting for him. I could've sat and relaxed in the car at his apartment, but he hasn't invited me into his space yet. He's let me around the clubhouse, however, and I have a feeling that with a man like Bash, it's significantly more important to him. I'd believe he lived at that MC if it weren't for him mentioning his apartment to me a couple of times and then having his car parked around the back of the buildings as well.

"I have our food in the oven." I offer an easy smile. It's all pretty domestic, and I'm not too sure how he'll take it. You hear those stories of the bad boys not liking to be tied down in any way, how they like the wild, inconsistent, playboy types. Could Sebastian be that way as well? His face lit up earlier when he saw me and then again when I told him I brought him some dinner. Maybe he's a bad boy without that particular bad habit. "If you want to come sit, I'll get you a beer?" I offer and gesture to the oversized farmhouse table. My cheeks heat, remembering how he had me on that very table.

"Mm," he hums. "I see you staring at that spot. I know you're thinking of me eating your pussy. Shit, I'm reminiscing over it too, baby."

"I couldn't forget it…even if I tried," I acknowledge, opening the fridge and leaning in to grab us a couple of beers. As I make my way over to him, he takes the bottles from me and twists the tops off. He hands me mine, and I flash him a soft look. That was sweet and unnecessary, yet he did it regardless. He's always doing thoughtful stuff like that. I don't doubt it for a moment that Bash is a badass, hardened one-percenter, but when it comes to me, he's just…different. That sounds so cliché, but it's the truth. I think it's what draws me to him so strongly. That and the fact he doesn't attempt to smother me like some men have done in the past.

He grins. "Nah, you don't want to forget that. It was too fucking good." He winks, making a giggle bubble up in my chest.

"I'm glad you're in a good mood. You looked a bit stressed when I pulled up at your club. Are things always so tense with you and Chaos?"

He shrugs, releasing a sigh. "He's my closest friend, my brother. It wasn't tense between us, just the subject we were discussing was. We both worry and look out for each other. We're family, and that's what you do."

I nod, enjoying that he's comfortable enough to open up to me. He's been fairly closed off on his club relations, keeping things more surface level when we mention the MC. It's usually during one of our quick lunches or when he's fixing something else that's broken on my car. "And he's worried about you?" I ask, curious, but not wanting to pry too deeply and have him shut down on me.

"I found out some shit today and had to keep him up to speed. In our lifestyle, shit's not always easy, Sweet Pea. Sometimes it gets ugly, and there's nothing we can do but come up with a plan."

I know the feeling, more than he realizes. Ever since my father's death, nothing has been remotely easy. The authorities tried to claim that my father's death was a suicide, that he'd gone bankrupt and was so depressed that he took his own life. I know what they say is all a big fat lie. The cops were being paid off to make it seem one way, when it was the opposite. My father lost all of his money; not that he was overly rich, but comfortable. He earned his money from working hard, then his life was stolen from him as well. He was murdered, and I figured out exactly who did it. I am my father's daughter, after all, and I've always been a little too smart for my own good. At least, that's what my father claimed many times over.

The oven beeps, the timer signaling that our food's been heating for ten minutes. I hop up to grab it, but Sebastian is right behind me, taking the hot pad from my hand. "I'll get these out, babe. You grab us some plates, yeah?"

"Okay," I give in, my heart warming a touch more at his willingness to help out. It's like he wants to protect me when he can, yet not tell me I can't do something. He doesn't attempt to snuff out the strong-willed woman that I am. He embraces it and compliments me with his own alpha personality.

"I didn't ask earlier when you mentioned the food. I sort of assumed I'd get you all night to myself. You got anything you gotta handle tonight?"

I shake my head. "I was hoping we'd hang out too."

"All right, then. This smells so fuckin' good. I still want to eat your pussy for dessert, though."

A laugh spills free. He is extremely talented with his tongue. "If you think I'll fight you on that, you're mistaken."

He matches my excited smile, a deep chuckle rumbling his chest. "Fuck, baby, you know a way to a man's heart. Food and the best tasting cunt I've ever had."

I shoot him a glower. "I'm going to pretend like you just said mine's the only pussy you've ever had."

His eyes widen, a booming laugh spilling free. "Shit, I kind of like you like this. You getting possessive is making me hard. You're so goddamn sexy, Angel; you know that?" His tone grows quieter with the endearment, his voice earnest.

I take a big bite of my food, not wanting to meet his serious gaze. He's intense, and I love it, so much so, that if I'm not careful, he'll consume my heart far too easily. I have to be careful in everything that I do, and Sebastian brings such a strong feeling of freedom with him that I find myself forgetting to have my guard up. Each time I'm with him, I open to him more and find myself wishing I could stay with him longer.

Like today, for instance. I'm always the last waitress to leave. I take on any last-minute customers and tips I can get. This evening, however, the moment my boss hinted at it being too slow, I volunteered to leave. I think everyone who was there was shocked to hear me speak up. No one protested, and I grabbed some food and left as soon as possible. I still haven't asked my boss about another job either. Instead, I find my thoughts consumed with my thoughtful biker I can never get enough of. If I work more, I'll be around him less, and that's something I don't want, no matter how badly I need the extra income.

We finish our dinner in comfortable silence. I'm doing the dishes, not paying attention to what Sebastian has his nose into until I hear my name being called from down the hall. I dry my hands on the dish towel and head for my bedroom, thinking it's time for his pussy sundae. "Sebastian?" I say when I don't immediately see him in my room.

"In here, Angel," he calls, and I spin around, back into the hall. He widens the bathroom door, and I notice him next to the tub. He's got a few candles lit, which is why I didn't see a light on in there when I passed by. "You gotta be sore after running around. I figure, you fed me, so now I'll make sure you get to relax."

A breath escapes me as I take everything in. It's so simple, yet one of the nicest things a man has ever done for me. "I haven't had a bath in a while. It sounds heavenly."

He beams and starts peeling his clothes off.

"Uh, what are you doing?" I take a step into the bathroom, sliding off my shoes and socks.

"I'm getting in with you."

My surprised stare meets his. "You're not too manly for baths?"

"Fuck no, and anyone who says different hasn't been punched in the ribs before. A hot soak with Epsom salt can do wonders for your body."

"You just keep surprising me," I admit, and he reaches out to peel my shirt off. I work on unbuttoning my pants while he reaches around to free me from my bra. This is what I was thinking of earlier about Sebastian. I could get used to this, him, and everything he does. He makes it almost impossible for me not to fall for him. I'm afraid that when the time comes for me to leave, I'll be so far invested with him that my heart will break in the process. It already shattered with my father's death. I'm not sure how much more I can take without completely losing myself in the process.

"Your body should be illegal," I murmur, casting my eyes all over him. The man is gorgeous.

"I could argue the same," he replies, holding my hand as I step into the hot water. He gets in behind me and sits first. With his hands on my hips, he directs me between his thighs. It's intimacy on an entirely new level. For some reason, the nakedness and the water makes me feel exposed to him. "Turn around, Savannah. I wanna see you when we talk."

"Okay," I whisper, sliding my body around until he captures me with his gaze. He leans forward, reaching for me, tucking my hair behind my ear, and I tilt my face into his touch. My body instantly reacts, my nipples tightening up. "Is this better?"

"Mm, much. I could look at you all day."

I bite my lips, staring at the water between us. His cock bobs between his thighs, the length impressive at half-mast. "That should come with a warning," I gesture, and he chuckles.

"So should your curvy ass."

I shake my head, laughing to myself. He's always got something quick to come back with, and they always somehow sound like a compliment to my ears.

"I wanted you relaxed 'cause I've got some shit to discuss with you."

"Okay," I drag the word out, my stomach spinning with curiosity.

"I don't know how you're gonna take it. I was talking it over with Chaos when you showed up."

My brow wrinkles. "You're kind of scaring me with the buildup. You mentioned the subject was tense earlier, what is it?" *I knew he was too good to be true. He's probably married or has a crazy ex-wife or something else just as alarming.* I already know about the drugs, and surprisingly, it doesn't bother me. I knew he wasn't a saint when I met him. He's good to me just the way he is, and I'm not going to try to change that part of him. The way I see his dealing is that it's not any of my business.

"Well, I told you this morning that I had shit to take care of for most the day."

I nod, remembering his words. It's one reason why I was a little unsure about just showing up at the MC. I didn't want him to think I was becoming clingy or anything. I could've texted him, I suppose but didn't think of it. I'm used to my phone being shut off and only using the minutes when it's absolutely necessary.

"Shit was business as usual." He leaves out the details, and while some may be nosey on his drug deals or whatever he was up to, I don't want to know. "When it was time to leave, though, some new information got me twisted up inside. A man had your photo."

My body locks up, ready to jump out of this water and run. His hands latch onto my arms, keeping me rooted in the tub. It's not hurtful, just weighted, silently telling me to hear him out. I can't help but freak out; there are too many people searching for me. "He said your father is looking for you."

Tears fill my eyes at the mention of my father. *Those bastards have no right to speak of him, to bring him into any more of this.* I shake my head, the drops spilling over. How dare they come to Sebastian, to mess with this small blip of happiness I've found and mess it all up. It's too soon. I didn't want to lose my biker already.

"I remembered when you told me your father was no longer alive, and it raised some red flags. This wasn't a decent man searching for you, quite the opposite. I saw through his lie as soon as it left his mouth."

My lip trembles. "M-my father is dead. I would never lie about something like that."

He nods, moving to wipe my tears away. "I know, baby, and I believe you. No one would break so badly over a person they love. If you weren't being real with me, I'd call you out on it. You have any idea who'd be looking for you, though?"

I bite my shaky lower lip and admit, "A lot of people, probably. None of them very nice."

"I figured so. Especially with that fucker's connections. I talked it over with Chaos, cause I ain't letting a motherfucker touch you."

My hands reach up, moving to hold his cheeks in my palms. "How can you be real? My life has been so hard since my father died, and then Heaven sent me you."

He shakes his head. "Nah, Sweet Pea, you're my angel; it's not the other way around. I'm dark to your light, but maybe…maybe that's why we crossed paths. You needed someone like me to protect your innocence."

"I'm far from innocent."

"Not in my eyes, Savannah. Let me help you with whatever you're dealing with."

I shake my head. I'd love nothing more than to not be in this alone. "If you knew everything, you wouldn't think of me the same way. I-I can't get into this with you right now, I'm sorry." I stand.

Sebastian follows suit, draining the water and grabbing a towel. He steps in front of me and pats the towel all over my body, drying me before himself. "It's fine. I can be patient. Until you're ready to tell me whatever it is, I'll be here to have your back regardless."

My lip trembles as I watch him towel off his insanely sexy nakedness. Sebastian had to be sent to me by my father, there's no other way I can explain the reasoning behind me meeting him. Then he comes across someone searching for me today during his business deal. It has to be some sort of fate intervening here. I just wish I knew the right move in all of this. "Thank you, Sebastian. These people…they're bad, and they want me dead. There's so much more I wish I could tell you…but I can't—not yet, anyhow."

"My life isn't as straitlaced as you probably think it is, either. I have plenty of demons; my club has demons. I can't share shit with you either, so I get it. I hope one day you'll find that you trust me enough to open up. I'd never let anyone hurt you. Jinx and I both told the guy that we'd never seen you before. I felt it was important to talk with you about it, in case you needed me to handle something for you."

I take his hand in mine, linking our fingers together and lead him to my bedroom. I want to be intimate with this man more than ever right now. He's not pushing me to divulge my secrets. He's not attempting to sell me out or smother me. Sebastian wants to help, to take care of me, and it's been too long since I've had someone on my side like that. It makes me want to worship him and never give him up. "Thank you. Those men…they can't find out where I am, or they'll hurt me. Probably kill me, actually," I state, leaving out the details of why they're hunting me down.

A possessive growl rumbles through his sculpted chest as I fall back on my bed, tugging him with me. His heavy cock falls in place between my thighs, rubbing against my clit. My legs react, spreading apart to wrap around his backside. I hate seeing him still peppered with bruises. It makes me wonder if he's still sore. Hopefully, they go away soon, and my man has completely healed again. I can't wait to see his stomach without the bruises. Not that he's any less gorgeous or anything. That's hardly the case.

"They won't touch you. You're always safe with me," he promises, and I lean up, taking his mouth with mine. The crazy thing is that I actually *feel* safe in his arms, like nothing can get to me with him at my side. He doesn't owe me in any way, and he certainly doesn't deserve the trouble that I'll bring his way if the wrong people discover he's taken my side in this battle. I'm also not stupid enough to reject his help and protectiveness over me. Lord knows I can't seem to beat the bad guys on my own.

"Fuck me, Sebastian," I beg, and he kindly obliges, thrusting his cock deep. It's what I need in the moment, to forget everything else in the world except for Bash, the badass vice president warming my bed. If only things were different, and I wasn't having to hide out knowing I'd eventually leave this place. Maybe then, I could fight to keep him long term.

He rotates his hips, his groin grinding against my sensitive bud. A whimper of pleasure breaks free, causing me to pull my mouth from his. I could get lost in his kisses, allow them to pull me under and drown me in the immense feelings they spread through my mind and body. He's the best I've ever had—there's no doubt about it. "So good," I moan, wanting to be consumed by him even more. I want him to take completely over so I can stop having to worry about anything and just live and be free.

He grunts in response, tucking his face into my neck. He breathes me in, then peppers kisses over my throat, leading to my breasts. With a hefty lunge, he sinks into me deeply, and I cry out. He trails his hand over my abdomen, moving up to pinch my nipples before bringing his hand to grip my throat. He squeezes just enough to make my eyes widen and seek out his gaze.

"Sebastian?" I sigh as his grin turns possessive. He holds my neck firmly, his hips moving in sync with my own. My pussy is sopping wet at him expressing his dominance. Controlling men aren't really my thing, but that's not what's happening right now. He's showing me that he's strong, that he's dominant enough to protect me and keep me safe. He can easily take life with his hands, yet he chooses to use them to offer me security. He gives me the peace of mind to relax and stop worrying about anything and everything.

My orgasm hits me with the next squeeze of his fingers, my moans elevating to shouts of ecstasy. I scream his name, and his cock explodes inside me. His hot cum shoots deep into my womb, rattling me to my core. I'm a shaking mess when my sexual high finally calms down, and I can concentrate on the throbs my pussy and his cock still continue to make. Our minds are sated with the rush of serotonin, but our bodies still cling to each other, seeking every last zing of sensation.

"Fuck, baby," he mumbles, nuzzling against my tender flesh. My throat will probably have some light bruising tomorrow, but that doesn't matter in the slightest to me. What's important is why those marks are there in the first place. Sebastian was staking his claim that no one will hurt me or take me from him. I've never felt safer or more cherished in my life. "I wanna make this permanent. Not trying to freak ya the fuck out or anything. You'll be in safe hands, having me sleeping next to you every night."

I roll away from him, showing him my back. I don't want him to see the fresh bout of tears filling my eyes and flowing down my cheeks. He probably thinks I'm a hot mess enough, I don't want him to see how emotional he's made me tonight. My back grows warm as he scoots in, putting his front to my body. His arm wraps over my waist, clamping down, holding me tightly to him. "Mean it, Angel. I don't fuck around when it comes to giving my word to someone."

I nod, swallowing. I speak softly, so my voice doesn't crack. "I want you here, Sebastian. I haven't wanted anything this badly in a long time. We did it again, though, had sex without protection. I need to remind you that I'm not on birth control." I can't go to the pharmacy for a refill in case my name pops up on anyone's radar. I didn't think about it before I left. I hadn't considered I'd meet anyone and I'd need it.

He presses a kiss to my temple, allowing me to keep my tears private. "I got you, Savannah. Stop fretting over what we've already done. Sleep, baby. Ain't no one coming after my woman tonight."

Bash

I take in his scent, his warmth, and the way he makes my heart feel full once more. It's no longer the crushed, empty feeling in my chest I'd grown to live with since my father was murdered. With Bash surrounding me, I close my eyes and finally sleep soundly.

Sapphire Knight

Bash

Chapter 10

She's gonna forever say "I got this" even with tears in her eyes.

- AW Camping

Bash

"You have another deal this week?" Chaos questions as I take the seat beside him. It's where I usually sit at the table. We had church earlier, yet he still hasn't left the room, taking time to hear out any personal shit the brothers need to speak with him about. I'm always here for them if they need me, too, but usually, it's only Chaos and Jinx who hit me up on a personal level.

I nod. "Maliki again. He's a persistent fucker, but I've been raking in some dough on these parties he throws. Same with Jinx."

"That's good news, brother. Tell me…he still asking after your woman?"

"Every week it's the same shit. We meet up, discuss the drop, and before we bounce, he asks me if I've seen Savannah. He's sticking to the same sob story about a distraught father on the search."

"Christ, the motherfucker's like a dog with a bone. How long has the questioning been going on now? A month or so?"

I release an irritated exhale, rapping my knuckles against the table. I need to do something with my hands while I talk about the thing that's been eating at me the most recently. Having anyone looking for my angel makes me punchy. I want to hit and ask questions later. I haven't, only because of the business I've got going with Maliki, or else I'd have laid his ass out and told him to get on down the road. "It's been eight weeks since the first time he's asked about her. Eight times, always with the same photo. I haven't wanted to stab someone this bad since we were cleaning up the clubhouse."

"Fuck, Bash, eight weeks. That isn't good, he's a bigtime shitbag. You know it as well as I do."

My muscles tense, more so than from a moment before. He's just confirmed my thoughts. I knew it in my gut, and hearing Chaos agree is like loading bullets in the chamber, knowing I'm about to pull the trigger and do the time. "She still hasn't told me fuck-all passed her father being dead. Sly found out about her dad for me. He confirmed that the old man's truly dead and Maliki is full of some fairy tale bullshit story. Not that I didn't believe my beautiful angel in the first place, but week after week of dealing product to him, I was beginning to wonder if I was fuckin' blinded by good pussy. Turns out Savannah's telling the truth, and I'm a goddamn dick for questioning her honesty. Her own father's death, and yet, I considered she could be milking me. Feeling real low right about now."

"You didn't know, so throw that mopey bull out the window. You did the right thing, watching the club's and your back, with a newcomer. That dirty pissant still has no clue she's yours?" Chaos mutters, before taking a swig of his drink.

"None that I know of, but she's been acting worse lately about things than when I first met her. Aside from the diner and the clubhouse, she won't leave the apartment. She ducks and practically sprints from the front door to the car. I've seen her leave the diner. It's the same thing there too. I'm worried about her being cooped up like she is. No one deserves to live like that. At least now I understand why she's such a recluse. Hell, without the threat hanging over her, I wonder if she's normally like that at all. I don't want my woman to be scared to go anywhere…ever, man. Makes me feel like I'm not doing enough for her. It's my responsibility as her man to make her feel safe, you feel me?"

"You need to talk to her, set her at ease. You've had time to get close with this chick. She may be willing to open up to you now. If she stays freaked out, maybe you can at least give her a little peace of mind when she's lost in her thoughts. I'm sick of seeing women hurt and taken advantage of. You know me, brother. That shit doesn't fly personally or with the club."

I agree with him completely. "I feel the same, I have you on that account." I consider his advice concerning Savannah. I can try, but there's no way to know if it will help or hinder our closeness. I shrug and admit, "She's headstrong, part of the reason I can't get enough of her. I don't want her stubbornness to get her killed or kidnapped or fuck knows what, when it comes to Maliki. His type is bad news."

Chaos gestures to the door, and I head out with him. He continues to talk as we stroll through the bar, eventually making it out front. The warm Georgia air surrounds us, the sun shining brightly, reminding me why I love the south. "Exactly. Put that shit on lockdown and make her tell you what you need to know."

I scoff. There's no way to make Savannah do *anything* she doesn't want to. I meant it when I said she's headstrong. The woman would starve to death before she let anyone see her face and that knowledge breaks my heart. "I'll figure out something. I have no choice. I need to know if this shit blows back—"

He interrupts, "You don't have to ask. We got you."

"Appreciate it, Prez." I offer him a chin-lift, reaching over to clap his solid shoulder. "I'm headed out. Savannah should be back at the apartment anytime."

"You two living together now, or you have your place still, too?"

"I showed up to her spot and never really left," I admit, and Chaos chuckles.

"You're a bastard. That little woman didn't stand a chance."

My shoulders bounce, not sorry in the slightest. He's right. Once I had my sights set on her, I'd decided she'd be mine, and she is. "She was stranded, and I'm not the type to turn my back on a stray. Especially not one that beautiful. See ya, man."

"Yeah, later." He sends me off with a nod, and I stride to my motorcycle. The engine rumbles loudly as I fire the powerful machine to life and kick the stand up. I toss him two fingers as I roll out of the parking lot, headed for home.

"Angel?" I rasp as I close the blue apartment door behind me. I know she's here; I saw my shiny Dodge Charger parked in her usual slot. It's become the new designated spot, but I don't mind in the slightest. I wasn't able to fix her old clunker—not that I tried too hard—so she's been driving mine when she needs it. It's safer than hers, anyhow, so it sets my mind at ease. I know it's stressful for her because she brings it up often that she needs to get a different vehicle.

She's nuts to worry about it. Hell, she has no idea, but I'd do much more for her if she'd allow me to. Never imagined when I fell for a woman that she'd be sweeter than peach cobbler. She's also kind, stubborn, and dead set on doing everything for herself.

"Sebastian?" she calls from the bedroom, sounding a bit more off than her usual sweet melodic voice. I eagerly make my way to the back of the apartment, more than ready to see her beauty and kiss her pouty lips to find her curled up in a tiny ball on the bed. I'd ordered us a king-sized about six weeks ago once I realized this wasn't going to fizzle out between us anytime soon. She was pissed, but I got her to give in once I demonstrated with her what we could do with the added mattress space.

My brow wrinkles with concern. This is new. She's always smiling and excited to see me when I come in. To find her looking so pale has me worried and on edge. "You all right, Sweet Pea? You sick or something?"

She groans, and the sound sends me straight to her side. My hand moves to her forehead to feel if she's overheated. "I've been better," she acknowledges. She takes a few deep breaths and admits, "It's been happening more frequently, but today was the absolute worst. Our daily special was liver and onions. It seemed like there were onions everywhere. I had to come back home. The smells at the diner were making me gag. If I served another plate, I was going to throw up."

"Fuckin' shit, woman. I told you that you work too damn hard. You should've called me; I could've driven you home. You need a break, baby. It's overdue. Those fuckers at the diner don't give two shits if they run you ragged for coffee refills and whatever else."

"Uh," she groans again, turning her face toward the bedspread. "Don't talk about coffee, please. I can still smell it, and I've been home for an hour already."

"That, too? Is it just food items, or any strong smells?"

"It's a mixture, but those are the worst so far."

I shake my head, rubbing my fingers through her soft hair that's spread in all directions. "Want me to get you some Sprite or maybe salted crackers? Would they help or mess it up more? You need me to pick up some meds? Tell me what to do for you, Sweet Pea."

Her glazy irises meet mine. "You're *so* good to me, Sebastian."

I nod. "Of course. You're my woman," I reply immediately without giving it any thought. I'd do anything to make her smile, to keep her happy and with me.

Her regard grows soft. "I'll be fine. I'm not sure if you will be when we talk about things, though."

My spine goes ramrod straight, not liking where this is heading one bit. Whatever Savannah has to say, she better not attempt to push me away. She did that shit in the beginning, refusing my help and then with her attempting to make us talk only about money for my bike. That was the last I wanted from her, and it hasn't changed. The only thing I was ever interested in, from the beginning, was getting to know her. Once I wiggled my way in, I couldn't stop there. I craved more of her. I still do. I want all of her—the good, the bad, the ugly. It doesn't matter as long as I get every piece of her.

I continue to rub my digits in her silky locks, reveling in how beautiful she is, even when she's not feeling well. This woman has another thing coming if she thinks she's going to give me up or that I'll let her go without one hell of a fight. She's become a constant in my life, day after day I come home to her. I'd never spent much time away from the club once I became a part of that world, always taking a club whore to warm my bed at night. Since Savannah, she's all I've been able to think about and truly desire to be around. She's made this place feel like a home, and that's where I yearn to be at night.

"You sure you don't need anything?" I inquire again, lying beside her. We're facing each other. I did it purposefully so I can watch my angel's expressions. Swear to Christ, Savannah better not break my damn heart. Lord knows, she could. She's my bright light after I went through the dark shit with Chaos and helping him clean up the club's messes. There were some rough times before shit got square, and then she came along out of nowhere. *She's my happy place, my woman.*

"I'm okay." She blows out another breath, and I smell the mint from her mouthwash. "Actually, having you here has made me feel a bit better. My stomach is still twisting, but more with anxiety and not the sickness."

"I make you anxious?" I hope it's that pitter-patter-heart sort of anxiety and not the bad one 'cause she's gonna give me the boot. I should've found a way to fix her car. Damn it. Savannah's the independent type, and it must be driving her crazier than I'd expected with me helping take care of her. She needs to realize I do everything because I want to, because I care for her, and because I can.

She swallows, and I press my mouth to her forehead. I don't want to overwhelm her, but damn, what if I can't kiss her in the future? I'll fight for her with everything I've got, but I can only do so much. If she doesn't want me, then I'm thoroughly screwed. I'm falling for this woman headfirst, and there's no way to pump the brakes. Christ, I've tried to. I was doing fine, living my bachelor lifestyle until I had a taste of her sweet little ass and then I was a changed man. Don't get me wrong, the club is still my life and it always will be. I still deal regularly too, because I have to make a living somehow. Selling dope may not be honorable in her eyes, but it's what I know how to do. Aside from hit shit and be the VP in the Kings of Carnage motorcycle club.

"Sebastian," she quietly utters with a sigh, reaching for me.

I scoot in closer, not giving an ounce of care if she's sick or not. I want to be near my sweet pea, to feel her presence against me. "Whatever it is," I declare genuinely, "Everything will be okay, baby. I'm here for you."

She sits up suddenly, getting to her feet. I'm thinking she's going to pop off and puke, but she begins to pace instead. I notice her face isn't as pale as it was when I walked in the door either, so it gives me a touch of comfort. "This is serious," she asserts, and I sit up again. I shift to the edge of the bed, ready to pounce on her if necessary.

"I'm pretty serious about you, beautiful. I can't emphasize it enough. How about you come out with it already, so we can handle whatever's eating away at you. I don't do suspense well; it makes me punchy, Angel."

My words lighten her mood a touch, throwing off her thoughts. She faces me, wearing a smirk. "I like you being punchy. Keeps things interesting, and you do a decent job at drywall repair."

I snort and roll my eyes. She's only seen me do one patch job, and it was from a bad day at work. I didn't take it out on her. I didn't even know she was at home when I lost my temper and punched a hole in the closet. Some shit fell when I was digging around, and it was my breaking point. I got into a fight with the wall and ended up patching it up a few days later. "Get over here and tell me what's up, Sweet Pea."

Savannah takes the few steps between us until her sweatpants covered legs touch my knees. Her tiny feet line up on the insides of my boots, and for some reason, that has my stomach flipping. I don't know what it is about this woman, but she has me feeling some type of way. Having her close again instantly calms me inside, and I can think straight once more.

She tangles her dainty fingers with mine, seeking my comfort. The differences between us are more than prominent. My hands are big, scarred, and tattooed, where hers are small, pale, and perfect. I'd never deny her anything, for that matter. I wait on bated breath for her to say whatever it is weighing heavily on her mind. I meant it when I admitted I don't do suspense well.

"I'm pregnant," Savannah confesses, with a shaky exhale. She's been carrying this alone, for who knows how long. I feel like a dick for not seeing her symptoms for what they truly are and offering her the help she obviously needs.

My jaw drops, my lips parting in shock. "I wasn't expecting that to leave your mouth, to be honest."

"It was bound to happen, Sebastian. We've been pretty careless. We've had lots of sex, and you haven't pulled out each time, and I didn't tell you too either. We're both at fault for not stopping to wear condoms and acting more responsibly. At some point, that's going to result in a baby."

I tug her to me, wrapping my arms around her. "You're right, Angel." I breathe the words. I'm just so damn happy she isn't trying to break it off and leave me. I never realized that was one of my worries until today. It really hit home with me about how much Savannah means to me. I pepper her with the first questions that come to me. "How are you feeling now? You still sick? How can I help make this easier on you?" *Why do I feel so enamored knowing she's having my child, and I'll be linked to her forever because of it?*

She leans back, meeting my gaze. Tears swim in her eyes. "I-I'm scared, Sebastian. I've been keeping a low profile, and that includes not going to the doctors. How can I have a baby if I can't go to a hospital for checkups? This is why I've been anxious. I don't have the answers to any of this, except to come out in the open."

I squeeze her a little tighter, wishing I could take her uncertain thoughts away and replace them with contentment. I tackle the largest issue first, pleased she's finally come to me with something I can fix. "The club has a doctor on standby. I can have him help out with that aspect. I can get you vitamins or whatever and bribe whoever I have to, if necessary."

She shakes her head, "That's not all, Sebastian. If it was only a doctor, I wouldn't be so freaked out. There's more, so much more. I haven't told you everything about my past, about what made me become so secretive."

"Talk to me, baby. I'm here for you. Not only do I care a fuck of a lot about you, but you're going to be the mother of my child. Tell me what else is messing with that pretty head of yours."

"I've been hiding...*crap*, it'll be so much harder to hide with a newborn. How can I raise a child in all of this?" It's spoken more to herself than me. It's like the thought hit her, and everything else faded away, including me. Her words strike fear in my heart, a sadness mixed with anger spirals through me, and I spit out the first thing that comes to my mind.

"So, what are you saying? You plan to kill it? You're gonna get rid of our kid without even explaining what the fuck's going on?"

Savannah gasps, the tears coming quicker and spilling over her flushed cheeks. "No, I-I was planning on telling you more about my circumstances, so you know what you're in for. Or, if you decide that you want me out of your life for good. I'd understand if you did." She sniffles, and a possessive growl rumbles my chest. *She's not going anywhere, and neither is our baby.* If I have to tie her sexy ass to the bed and hand feed her until she gives in, then I'll do what it takes to make her see me more clearly.

"That's the last fucking thing I want. I care about you, and now I'll be caring about the baby as well. I'll repeat myself however many times I have to-to make you believe me. I'm in it for the long haul, babe, there's no turning back now. We've created a life. Now, tell me, Savannah. No more procrastinating. I can shoulder some of that burden you've been hauling around. Let me do it; let me be your man."

She hiccups, her free hand swiping at her wet cheeks. It kills me to see my sweet angel such a mess over this shit. "You already know my father died, but there's much more to that story that I've kept to myself."

"All right, let's hear it." I hold her to me as I sit on the bed, her body securely resting in my lap. There's no way in hell I'm going to allow her to run off if she suddenly decides to try.

"My father, his death…it was all cold and calculated. He was murdered after his bank accounts were drained."

"No shit? I'd been putting pieces together, but to have you say that aloud, it solidifies things a bit more."

Tears trail down her flesh as she quietly sobs. My heart breaks for my woman. I want to take her pain inside and swallow it away. "After I discovered him, I lost it a little. I couldn't let this heartless killer get away with what he'd done. I started looking into him, and I quickly realized there were many other deaths related to him. He was a greedy pig, hiring people to work with him then stealing their money from underneath their noses. My father found out what he was doing and was killed for it."

"Christ," I huff as the depth of her situation begins to rear its ugly head.

She continues. "I-I came up with a plan, and I found the murdering sicko. I made sure we crossed paths."

"Fuck, baby." I exhale, clenching my fists at the thought of her safety being in jeopardy. She's too brave for her own good. He could've killed her as well, and I'd have never gotten the chance to know this amazing woman.

"He let me get close to him—as close as I could stomach in the short amount of time. He was so arrogant, believing he was untouchable, and I just…I hated him with every breath I took." She meets my gaze, and I can tell I'm not going to like what she has to say next.

I grit my teeth, bearing down for the oncoming blow, whatever it may be.

"I seduced him," she whispers, making my eyes clench closed as thoughts race in my mind. Imagining her with another man makes me want to hurt someone badly. "I fucked him," she acknowledges afterward, and I bite down so hard, I swear I'm going to crack teeth.

She's mine.

"Then I killed him," Savannah concedes.

My eyes fly open to meet hers. "Angel, did I hear that right, or did I imagine what I wanted you to say?"

Her head tilts, taking me in. "I-I admitted to killing him. I did it in cold blood, premeditated. I planned it all out, step by step and went through with it." Her lip trembles, as more sobs wrack her chest. "I'm so horrible. Now you see why his family wants me dead. Why I have to hide and why this child will be in jeopardy if I seek medical care. I can't let them hurt our kid."

"There's not a bad bone in your body, you hear me?" I reassure her because it's the goddamn truth. If she had any idea about the situations I've handled myself—well, she wouldn't be judging herself so harshly.

"I wish I could believe that," she murmurs and swallows tightly, staring toward the ground.

I move, lifting her chin. I want her eyes back on me. "I won't let anything happen to you, not to either one of you. I can handle this, and if I need some help, my club will have my back. Me and Chaos…well, you know we're close. He's my best friend, means more to me than blood. He'd step in if I needed him to. As would Jinx, Sly, North…all of 'em. The prospect I have on you would even lay down his life." *He better, anyhow,* I quietly growl to myself.

"But why? It's not like we're married, and I'm not naïve enough to believe someone would help me from the goodness of their hearts. Not with something this serious and deadly to bite them in return."

I shake my head. "Nah, Sweet Pea. They'd help because you mean the fucking world to me, and they're my brothers. That means something to us. They hear you're having my kid, and they won't even question as to why this is priority for me."

"I wish I had people who cared for me like that."

"You do," I murmur, pressing a kiss to the tip of her nose. "You've got me."

Bash

Chapter 11

Expecting things to change without putting in any

effort is like waiting for a ship at the airport.

- @functionalrustic

Savannah

I've got him. Bash says it without a second thought, and then I'm a blubbering mess for an entirely new reason. I just admitted my darkest secret aloud, and he's not running for the hills. He's doing the opposite, actually. He's offered to help me and is already being protective over the teeny tiny life growing inside my belly. Out of all the bikers to meet on the side of the road…I met him. It has to be my father intervening from above. That's the only reasonable explanation I can come up with to explain how someone like Sebastian, with a big heart, good character, and fierce protectiveness, was sent to me when I needed him the most.

"You would do that for me? You'd risk your life without another thought?"

His steady gaze beats down on me. "Of course, you don't even have to ask. I would've protected you regardless of you having my child or not.

I'm glad you told me…I only wish you'd felt comfortable enough to open up to me sooner. I could've done something about it a long time ago. I can only imagine the pressure and stress you've been under this entire time."

"I-I never know who's working for him. It seems like that family has a way of sticking their hands in everything. I may not be in your business or around you at the club a lot, but you don't have the same evilness in your heart. I trust you. I had to be sure of it before I told you."

He grunts. "I take it this influential family you're afraid of has to do with Maliki, and that's why he's been asking Jinx and me each week if we've seen you before."

I bite my bottom lip and nod. My tears are finally beginning to dry up. I'm sure I look like a hot mess with bright pink, tearstained cheeks, and red-rimmed eyes. I hate it when I cry. Lord knows I've done my share in the past year with everything that's happened. "Maliki is his brother…the man I killed."

"*Fuck, baby,*" he breathes, rubbing his hand over his brow. "Maliki's a dangerous scum bucket. I'm so fucking proud of you for hiding out this long and staying alive. You did the right thing keeping to yourself, but staying so close to ATL is risky."

"It's cowardly, and I didn't have much money," I comment with a sigh.

He jostles me, arguing, "The fuck it is. You're the bravest bitch I know. I think that's why I respect you so damn much."

My heart fills, knowing he thinks of me that way, that he respects me. "I think you're pretty great, too, Bash."

He growls. "That road name is for my club, Angel. I'm *your* Sebastian."

I nod because he's right. "You *are* mine."

"Damn straight," he agrees, pressing a searing kiss to my mouth. "I don't want you worrying over this shit anymore. I mean it. I'm gonna have a chat with my brothers to get them up to speed a bit more and come up with a plan. I'll make sure Maliki never bothers you again. You have my word."

"You said it yourself, he's dangerous. I would never forgive myself if anything happened to you. I don't think I could handle it."

"So am I, Angel, more than you realize. You keep doing your thing, you go wherever you need to, and take the car. I have a prospect on ya, in case you need something."

It's my turn for my mouth to drop open. "I'd seen a biker I didn't recognize around, but I didn't know he was there for me. I just put two and two together…that's what you meant earlier when you said the prospect would protect me with his life."

He shrugs, not perturbed with me linking it all together. "I've had him on ya for a while. Wanted to make sure you didn't catch any blowback or anything for being affiliated with the club. The prospect hasn't seen anyone following you or anything like that, so I think you're still in the clear around here. I don't want you overstressing yourself about this. You're pregnant and need to take it easy, on everything. You need something, you text me or flag down the prospect. I don't care if it's a candy bar you're craving. All you gotta do is ask. I'm here for you now, and KOC will be as well."

"So, this entire time, you've been trying to help me and protect me, huh? But why me?"

"Haven't you figured it out yet, Sweet Pea?"

I bite my bottom lip, my stare filling with heat as this man worms his way further into my heart with each sentence. "What's that, VP?"

"I'm a goner for you. I haven't been able to get you off my mind since the moment I opened my eyes on the side of the road to meet yours. I knew then I had to have you, that you were my angel. Getting to know you, I discovered that not only are you empathetic and genuine, but you're considerate, headstrong, intelligent, and the best woman I've ever met. It also helped that you're fine as fuck. Now you're pregnant with my kid, and damn, baby, it's fate. What are the odds that two people will break down and wreck in the dark, at the same time, and be thrown together like we were?"

"I'd say not many, at least not unintentionally. I could imagine it being a setup, but I had no clue you'd be there that night over two months ago, or that my battery cable would come loose."

"Exactly. We were meant to be. I know it already; I'm just waiting on you to get on board with me."

A quiet snicker leaves me as he smirks. He's pretty proud he's figured this all out and I'm having to catch up. Not that I mind one bit. Sebastian is someone I've needed most in my life this past year and had no clue. "I'm on board now…sorry to keep you waiting," I tease.

He winks, flashing me a grin, looking even sexier now that his mood seems to be lifting. "Not gonna lie, thought you were giving me the boot. You had me sweating."

I laugh loudly at seeing him exhale in relief. "Oh, please, there's no way I could leave you, Sebastian. Not anymore. I'm in too deep. I may've considered it in the beginning. I tried warning myself to be safe and hold back from getting in too deep with you, but that thought is gone."

"Thank God," he rasps, moving to peel my shirt off. "These perfect tits are gonna swell, and I can't wait to suck and fuck 'em, Baby. You're already the most beautiful woman I've ever seen, but imagining you rounded out with my kid, makes me want to come in my pants."

"How about you come in me instead?" I suggest, squirming my way free to crawl over the huge bed toward the pillows. At least when he ordered the new bed, he had enough sense to order sheets and a comforter the same shade as my old set.

"Mm, you feeling well enough for me to ravage you? Not trying to make you uncomfortable when you're sick. Sex can wait, Angel. I'll be patient for you."

I wiggle my eyebrows, licking my lips at the thought of him ravishing me. "More than all right. I'm feeling extra horny for my man…for my baby daddy." The swirling emotions that were plaguing me when he arrived have passed. I haven't felt this at ease in a long time, and there's nothing I'd enjoy more than having him closer. I want to feel him all over me.

He groans loudly. "You can call me daddy all fucking night, Savannah. I'll make your sexy ass come so many times you pass the fuck out."

"Sounds perfect to me," I retort, my body igniting in response. Sebastian reaches for my ankles, tugging my yoga pants down my legs and tosses them behind him toward the closet. I may have a thing about stuff being everywhere and he's been good so far about trying not to leave clothes strewn about. He's a man, though, so there're T-shirts often left in random spots around the apartment. Drives me crazy to find them when I clean up, but I'd miss them if they were gone completely.

His tattooed hands trail up my thighs, his fingers grabbing for my panties next. I'm already panting in anticipation as to what's to come. He never disappoints or leaves me needy. The man knows how to satisfy like no other. "You have too many clothes on," I point out, wanting him naked as well. I love his body and can never get enough of rubbing my hands all over him.

He shrugs. "The only thing I need to worry about is pulling my cock out enough to stick it in your warm, wet cunt. I'm not all pretty and curvy in the right spots like you."

I offer a grin and argue. "Not so fast. I want to see skin. You know I like to look at you."

He smirks, his cobalt irises sparkling. "You will, only it'll be your skin on display. Now hush up and let me eat this tasty pussy."

"Oh, Lord!" I nearly shout as his mouth meets my core, and his firm grip digs into my hips. I've concluded that this man is insatiable where my vagina is concerned. I don't mind, even though it's what got us pregnant in the first place. He's too good. I won't tell him that and stroke his ego any further. Right now, he's hot and humble, and I don't ever want that to change.

"Can't get enough of you, Sav."

Thank God for that.

"I don't mind," I sigh, as I fall a little deeper for Sebastian. I'm already in-lust with him, but his understanding and willingness to protect me has me feeling more on the *in-love* side. I can feel the hooks sinking their way into me, linking me to him more than before. I was already crazy about him; now, we're having a baby together, and he covets even more of me. It requires one heck of a man to be that decent and strong. He'll take on all my weight and not even blink over it. "Please, don't ever stop." I breathe the plea. He probably thinks I'm talking about him licking me so thoroughly, but I'm not.

"Not planning on it. If you can talk this much, then I'm not doing a proper enough job," he growls around my center, sending pleasurable tremors through me to the point my toes curl.

I release a throaty laugh, knowing how completely wrong he is. I can barely think, let alone expect him to do better. I gasp as he flattens his tongue against my clit and moves it in circles. Anyone can do that with their fingers, but with a tongue? *Holy wow.* "Seb," I cry as my pussy pulses, attempting to grip anything close enough to my opening. "I want you!"

"You got me, baby," he rasps, repeating his earlier sentiment and ravaging me until I'm a whimpering mess. I come fast, because, let's be real, there was no way for me to fight off that type of assault.

He crawls up my frame like some sort of panther man, and it's beyond sexy. How he effortlessly has this much swagger has me thrown for a loop. Maybe some people really are born with it while others, like me, struggle with being sexy. He pushes my shirt up, cupping my breasts through my bra. He rasps, "You warm enough for me to take this off?"

My heart squeezes at his thoughtfulness. I'd mentioned it randomly one day that the cold hurts my nipples and he must've paid attention to my complaining. "Mm, I'm burning up. You have me on fire," I smile cheesily, and he chuckles. That deep timbre has my pussy clenching. "Fuck me, Sebastian. Stop making me wait to feel you inside."

"With pleasure," he murmurs as his lips come to graze mine. He reaches down to tug his zipper and button open on his jeans, then he's jerking his dick out. In the next breath, he's rubbing the head of his cock up and down through my wet slit. I'm soaked, to the point it'd be embarrassing if I didn't know how much he enjoys it. "Let's see how much of my cock this hot, wet cunt can take today."

"All of it. Give it all to me."

"You asked for it, and I'm a man who pleases." He slams home, jarring me up on the massive bed. With his long body, we needed the added space, and it has its perks during sex as well.

"Harder," I demand, and he thrusts quick and deep. "Yes!"

His hips gyrate, causing little spasms to shoot through me everywhere. Sweat peppers his brow, his gaze remaining locked on mine. His irises have darkened immensely, going from their playful sparkle to resembling the dark depths of the ocean. Gone is his easygoing nature, and in its place, is a man on a mission.

"Feels so fuckin' good," he grunts, and I hum in agreement.

He's everything to me—warmth…comfort…home. I tuck my face into his throat, sucking and licking a trail to his lobe. I nibble and groan in his ear; it always drives him wild with lust. He responds with quick jolts from his hips. His hand slides down the back of my thigh, hiking it up higher against his side. The new position gives him enough room to tilt my hips wider and slide in deeper and rougher. His length strums my pussy, back and forth, rubbing against my G-spot.

My eyes roll back, and a long, loud moan leaves me breathlessly. "I'm close."

"Me too…not coming until you do."

His hand leaves my thigh, sliding under to squeeze my ass cheek. It has my groin tilting up to meet each thrust from him. He continues his exploration, his fingers dipping between my cheeks until he finds my secret hole, puckered and waiting. His fingers gather some wetness running below my pussy, then he's thrusting them into my ass. Pleasure explodes through me, and I scream, my orgasm hitting me full force. I pretty much black out as I wail and thrust my hips at him to fuck me as hard as he possibly can while I ride out my tidal wave of bliss. Pregnancy hormones are no joke because I feel the rush tenfold.

"Angel, Jesus, you feel so perfect," he groans as he floods my core with splatters of warm cum. I never would've imagined the sensation of him filling me up like that would feel so flippin' good, but it does. His hands come to the sides of my head, tangling in my hair as his mouth seeks mine. Sebastian's tongue dips inside, solidifying our mating, and it couldn't be any more perfect. It's exactly what I needed after having such a serious conversation with him. He makes me feel cherished and protected, and those feelings aren't easy to come by.

He gently lifts off me, laying to my side. His cock hangs out, coated in our combined wetness. For some reason, it's sexy to me. I kind of want to lean down and lick him clean, but I don't. Not after my stomach was so upset. I'm a little edgy about putting anything else in my mouth at the moment. "I didn't hurt you, did I?" he asks, pressing several kisses to my temple and hair.

A giggle bursts free. I can't help it. I've read a few stories about how some men become overly worried and doting when they discover their other half is pregnant. I can already see Sebastian being one of them. It's ironic how one little stick from a gas station can completely change your life. Murder changed mine in a blink, and now, new life has altered it once again. I'm thankful for this gift, as that's what this baby is.

"What's so funny?" he rasps, wearing a sated grin. He rubs his hand over his head, ruffling up his messy hair. *How can men do that, and it only makes them look better?*

"You…worrying if I'm okay after our great sex, and remembering all the acrobats you've had me pulling over the past few months."

He chuckles, and the sound reverberates deep. I love it. It makes me feel all warm and fuzzy inside. "I may have an adventurous appetite. Luckily, you know how to fill it."

"That's putting it lightly. Not to mention you like eating me out in random places. Who knew your Charger's back seat would have enough room to do the things you've done to me in it?"

"I haven't heard you complain—quite the opposite actually. And obviously, the car was a good buy, even if it was only for the back seat."

I roll my eyes because he's totally right. "I enjoyed every minute of it. I was just thinking that some men become sorta overprotective and worried when women become pregnant, and you're already showing signs." I rub my fingertips over his tattooed biceps. It tickles him, but if I stop, he'll nudge me to keep going. I love that little detail about him.

"Fuckin' right. I'll protect you with my last breath if needed, and I wanna know what I can do to make things easier on you during this pregnancy. I'm not one of those assholes who'll turn the other way and not care about you or that kid. We're a team. I'm responsible just as much as you are for that life. You're growing our baby in your tummy, so you need to be taken extra care of during that time as well."

My eyes grow watery. I can't help it; he's seriously the sweetest man I've ever met. I think it really drives home with me because it's not a bunch of pretty words with him. He's genuine, and that makes all the difference.

"You keep saying things like that, Sebastian, and my heart won't have a chance against you."

"That's the plan, Sweet Pea. Never gonna give you up. Now, let's take a nap, 'cause I've gotta come up with a plan to keep you two safe. Tomorrow, the only thing I want you worrying about is making a list of all the baby stuff we're gonna need. I'm gonna do this the right way with you, Savannah."

I release a sigh, snuggling into his arms. Just being here like this makes me feel safe. I watch his chest rise and fall with each breath, and the movement lulls me into a deep, sated sleep.

Sapphire Knight

Bash

Chapter 12

Let it hurt. Let it bleed. Let it heal. And let it go.

- Nikita Gill

Bash

"Shit is seriously fucking fucked," I complain to the table. We're in church. Chaos called for it once I informed him what was up. I had to confide in him over the confession Savannah shared with me yesterday. It was too big and important to keep it quiet and attempt to handle it alone. Especially with Maliki being involved. That complicates things on a whole other level. "I'm going to kill him," I vow to the men surrounding me. "Won't stand for him hurting my woman."

"So, you're finally claiming her?" North asks as he stares me down, not saying anything about the shit I just spilled on all of them about Savannah murdering a billionaire psychopath. That piece isn't what worries me, nor the others. The key in this situation is that Maliki is seeking retribution, and that could turn up some shit if he knows we're hiding her.

Jinx scoffs. The big Samoan casts North a glance and says, "He's been practically pissing on her leg from the moment she showed up here."

Sly snickers, his jade gaze twinkling. "She'd bust his balls if he tried. Wouldn't want to miss seeing that."

Chaos grunts his agreement. My woman has made her stubbornness known to the club. I fucking love that about her. She's a strong bitch. Although she'd have to be, for me to feel this way about her.

I shoot a glare around the table. They may be right. Doesn't mean I'm going to roll over and take the ribbing right now. I'm too worried about how this is all going to play out, to joke with them. After a beat of silence, I sigh, raking my hands through my hair. "Yes, I am claiming her. Savannah's pregnant."

A few mouths drop in surprise. The prez speaks up. "She's family. Nothing to question. We protect each other, and we protect our women." We voice our various agreements. "We've got to be smart about this, so it doesn't blow back and hit the club too hard. We're finally on the right side of building the club back up. We can't allow this rich fuck to drag us back down to square one."

North sits forward, his fists clenched on the table before him. "I can handle it. I'm the enforcer. I should be getting my hands dirty…not our VP."

I nod his way, acknowledging his loyalty and being grateful he feels I've earned it. "I couldn't ask you to take care of my personal problem, brother. It's not right."

It's Sly's turn to argue. "Doesn't matter. You're our VP. We gotta look out for you and the prez…it's what we do." He's the treasurer, but also a trained fighter. Facing things head-on for his brothers is part of his personality. I respect him a hell of a lot for it too.

Jinx huffs. "We're a team. We handle this together. Same as we've done in the past. It's how none of us winds up hurt, and shit gets taken care of swiftly and effectively."

Prez raps his knuckles on the table. "Agreed. Not letting you go rogue and wind up dead. Also not putting this off on one brother to handle either."

I sit back in my chair, knowing I've lost. If we vote on it, then my brothers will outvote me. It's in our nature to want to take up for each other. We've been around each other for too long through enough to be any different. "All right, any suggestions on how we go about this? I'm still killing him," I mutter petulantly.

Jinx shakes his head, used to me getting pissy and punching fuck sticks until they stop breathing. I warned Savannah that she didn't know what demons were. Lord knows I have my fill after becoming tight with Chaos. I wasn't good by any means before we grew close, but I did my fair share of torture once he told me what his plan was with the club. We worked side by side, doling out consequences, as he was the enforcer back then, and I was a new member. There was no way I was going to do nothing and allow my buddy to possibly end up dead. He tried to keep me out of it at first, but I wouldn't have it, and eventually, he brought me into the fold with him. He's my family. Not by blood, but by choice, and family protects each other.

"We use the weekly drop to our advantage," Jinx begins. "Maliki only has a few guys with him, so there will be less interference and chance for him to escape."

North's deep voice cuts through my thoughts. "Do we know he's at the top? We need to cut the head off the snake, or more will follow in his place."

I've looked into Maliki as much as I could without raising flags. When you're in the drug business and deal in the amounts of product that I do, you learn who your buyers are. Ignoring who they may be only asks for trouble and complications. I've been at this for too long to fuck up and get thrown in jail. I like my freedom and my cash more than being lazy.

"I have some intel on him, but not much. His brother is dead, obviously, so he's out of the picture. The mother died when they were young, and as far as I know, his father is old and not in the public much. I only know about his family based on the bio on his site and then a basic search. We may be able to dig deeper, but I don't think we'll find much more. Maliki seems to enjoy having full control over his business as well as other people. I don't see him being the type to have a partner who wasn't blood-related."

Jinx concurs. "I thought the same thing."

I nod, looking back at North. "I didn't want to tip him off that I was looking into him, so I kept it brief."

"I'll see what I can find out. A few of my contacts may have some dirt on him we can use," he murmurs.

The pensive man at my side runs his thumb across the gavel. He's thinking; I can see it all over his face. "You think it'll tip him off if you add a few brothers to this week's run? Maybe get him used to seeing more than you two? Or do you believe he'll bring more backup as well?"

I shake my head. "He's been the overconfident type from the moment I met him. He knows too many prominent people in Atlanta and everywhere else. He thinks he's untouchable. His brother was the same way, and now we know how he was killed. It took a woman sliding her way in and taking him out. She was probably the last person he ever expected to kill him."

"How'd she kill him?" North questions and I release a tense breath.

I don't enjoy thinking of Savannah with another man one bit. I'm not stupid enough to believe she hasn't been with several guys in the past, but I still don't like it. "She made sure he was relaxed enough to fall asleep. Stabbed him in the throat with a scalpel."

"Fuck," Jinx coughs, his eyes going wide. That was my reaction too.

"Not many women can get that personal. Usually, they go for the silent killers, like poison," Sly comments, and I nod. We know this. It's our job to be aware of what to watch out for to stay alive in this life. Bitches can be just as ruthless as men, and if they've been scorned, then even more so.

Chaos breathes, "She's strong."

"Mm. More than you know, brother."

He nods, and I can't help but feel pride that my brothers see Savannah for the bad bitch she truly is. "All right, for your deal this week, take Jinx, Sly, and a prospect with you. Get Maliki warmed up to the thought of you having a few more men on board. If he mentions it, tell him we've heard the gangs are getting restless toward the MC, since we've changed some of our allegiances. It's none of his fuckin' business what we do, but that'll make him think you're stupid enough to be comfortable with him to mention a little club unrest. He'll see us as being vulnerable, which is what we want."

North rasps, "He won't view us as a threat, and we'll take him down swiftly."

"I can do that. Jinx and I ride out again on Tuesday to go over Friday's order and delivery details. He never wants the product until it's right before one of his parties. The fucker's smart on that account."

Chaos flips the gavel over, mentioning, "Shame…it'd be too easy to tip off a rookie cop with a hard-on for justice. It'd be a career-making type of bust."

I shake my head. "The cop would end up dead, and whoever needed to would be paid off. Besides, Maliki doesn't even ride in the same vehicle on Fridays. He has his people load the product and take it. His pockets run deeper than any other buyer I've had before. That's why I had to pull Jinx in to help fulfill the order requests. Maliki buys twice to three times what my supplier can get without involving the Columbians."

Sly runs his hands over his head, exhaling. "Definitely need to make sure the fucker is dead, or he'll undoubtedly squirm his way back for revenge."

"Agreed," we all say, mirroring each other with the word and tense expression.

Chaos takes a swig of his drink and says, "It's settled. We've come up with an initial plan. Once we warm him up to our numbers, we'll revisit and discuss the next step. We have to keep this shit nonexistent to our other contacts if you know what I mean."

We grunt out acknowledgment, and the prez slams the gavel down, calling an end to church. My hand falls to his shoulder as I stand, squeezing it. I'm grateful for him calling church to discuss what Savannah and I are up against. He didn't even hesitate to have my back, and that's more than I could ever ask for. "Hit me up if you need me," I say, pushing my chair in. Chaos will be in here speaking to the brothers for a while, I'm sure.

I make my way to the bar for a shot. I need it after the discussion we had. Never thought I'd care for a woman, or anyone for that matter, as much as I do my woman and my future kid. The brothers know she's mine, so I don't have to be a jealous fuck around them with her, though I don't know if I can help it. I want all her attention on me. I'm too spoiled with her already. "Vodka," I bark in the prospect's direction and wait. I set my bottle of Sprite on the bar and scoot my ass onto a barstool.

When I left earlier, Savannah was feeling good, getting ready for work. I don't want her to bother with the diner, especially while Maliki is on the hunt for her, but the woman is determined to make her own money. I try calling Savannah, but she doesn't answer. I shoot her a text instead.

Wanted to check in. You feel all right and make it to work?

She doesn't respond, but that's fine. I know she will whenever she's not busy. That's another thing that I like about my angel—she's respectful, and in a relationship, that's important. I'm hoping after our long talk that she'll start to confide in me more and let me know when she's not doing so hot. I made her promise me this morning she'd call if she got sick again so I could come get her. Of course, she's capable of taking care of herself, but she shouldn't have to, because she has me. If all I can do is drive her home from work and get her some crackers, I'm going to do it.

My phone lights up, but it's still not my woman. It's my parents, or, more specifically, my mom. If I'm speaking to her, then I'm basically talking to my dad at the same time. She's notorious for reading him all my messages or putting me on speakerphone if she calls. I left her a brief message saying I had some news for her. I'm surprised it's taken her this long to get back to me.

Today must've been a farmers' market day for them. My mom makes homemade, organic, and gluten-free, or whatever dog treats. I thought she was joking when she first told me, but apparently, it's a thing, and the town's dogs love her biscuits. I grew up a few hours away from here. They still live in the same town and the same house. It's comforting when I go visit, but also weird, like being thrown back in time.

"Yeah?"

"Is that how you normally answer your phone?" My mom chirps, and I chuckle.

"I knew it was you."

"Well, all the more reason to say *hello, mother dearest*."

I release an amused snort. "Is Dad with you?"

"He sure is, did you want to speak to him instead?"

"Nah, I can let you know, and then you can relay it."

"Okay, Sebby, you're on speakerphone."

Of course, I am. "I've got a woman, and we're having a baby."

It's so quiet, you could hear a pin drop on the line.

After a beat, my mom says, "Uh, I think I misheard you…say again."

"I'm seeing someone, and she's pregnant. Kid's mine."

My dad speaks first. "Well, shit. Congrats, son!"

"A baby?" my mom breathes, her voice full of excitement and most likely shock.

"Yep, I'm gonna give my woman a few weeks to get in with the doc and whatnot, but then I suppose we should head up there so she can meet you both."

My dad's easy. "Sounds good. Love you, son."

"Love you too, Dad. Mom? You good?"

My dad speaks again. "She's crying, son. I think you just made her whole day. I'll have her give you a call back once she's settled down."

"All right, then, give her a hug from me. Talk to you soon."

"Bye, Bash." My dad respects the road name. It's my mom who won't give up my childhood nickname. I don't mind, though; the woman did birth me.

I hang up and sigh. One of the club whores sidles up to me, and I shoot her a glance. "You have any kids?"

She shakes her head. "Nope and don't want any. You don't have to worry about me sabotaging the rubbers."

My eyes grow wide at her statement. Sure as fuck hope none of the other club whores that show up get the itch to fuck up a condom around here. There's no telling how the brothers would react to that shit. "My woman's having my kid. I don't need any other pussy but hers," I grumble in response.

She bats her eyelashes, pushing her chest out. "I could suck you off, I like swallowing cum."

I hear the prospect choke behind me at her words, but they do nothing for me. "How about you be quick and quiet and go behind the bar. Prospect could use a blow job." I stand, ready to get the fuck out of here and see Savannah. I want to kiss her belly and then fuck her until she's satisfied.

"Th-thanks, Bash," he stammers out, eager to finally get a piece of the club's pussy. Prospects aren't allowed to touch any of the women unless we allow it. I'm not going to fuck this one, and the brothers are preoccupied, so may as well give the prospect something to be happy about. One day he'll get sick of the gash; it happens to us all. Once I had Savannah's cunt, there was no going back.

"Chaos comes out, you let him know I went home," I grumble as the whore sinks to her knees, and his eyes roll.

Bash

I'm only on my Harley for a few minutes when the turnoff to my apartment comes up. I picked this place specifically because of its location to the clubhouse. I notice the black SUV immediately. It's completely out of place. The large vehicle is parked behind my Charger, blocking it in and not parked in an actual slot. There's a man in a suit standing solemnly beside the driver's door with his arms crossed over his chest. I don't know who he is, though, he's not familiar in any way.

As I slow down enough to make the turn to the right, I notice another dude posted up beside the front door of Savannah's apartment. It's closed, but there's no denying the guy is definitely on guard. I recognize that fucker. He's the one who rides bitch in Maliki's vehicle when we meet up each week.

Fuck, fuck, fuck.

Rather than pull in right up front and go in guns blazing, I make my way toward the back of the lot. With any luck, they'll be distracted and think I live in another unit that I don't care who the fuck they are. That couldn't be further from the truth, however, as they're a threat to my family.

I have an idea on how to get to Savannah, I just need to give my prez a heads-up before executing it. I quickly ride around the turn to the back building of apartments where my place is. I skip the parking lot, driving up the handicap slope on the sidewalk. I come to a stop on the pathway leading to my place and shut my bike off, kicking the stand down. I swiftly hop off, digging my cell out of my pocket to quickly shoot off a text to Chaos.

Maliki's at Savannah's place. Goin' in.

The group text we're in used for emergencies and church vibrates multiple times as all my brothers respond. I don't check what they have to say, just shove the cell back in my pocket as I run inside my old apartment, slamming the door behind me. They'd more than likely tell me to wait for backup or not to go in at all, and I can't do that. As far as I'm concerned, each minute is another wasted sixty seconds to save my angel.

I jog toward the back of the apartment to my kitchen, yanking open the door to my freezer for my stash. I've got weapons and ammo in here, and the cooler turned off. I also keep some product in the drawer under my stove for emergency buyers. I know what you're thinking, and I don't cook here, so it's all good. Besides, I figure people are less likely to look in my freezer when searching for shit, versus my bedroom or whatever.

I grab for three knives, strapping them on, then reach for my two Beretta 92X Full-Size Semi-Automatic Pistols. I like them because they're lightweight and powerful enough that even Savannah can use them if necessary. The Berettas hold plenty of bullets and have a quick release feature for a fast magazine swap, though I did modify and switch out the plastic guide rod for a steel one. I have no idea how many men are in that apartment, and I need access to a lot of ammo, but also not be weighed down in case I need to fight. I'm planning on killing every motherfucker that showed up to hurt my baby.

I snatch an extra two full magazines, shoving them in my pockets. I strap one gun to my thigh for easy reach and carry the second. There's no time to give this any extra thought, as I don't know if Maliki will kill her inside or take her someplace else. How he fucking found her is beyond me. I can't help but feel partially at fault over this. If I hadn't fucked my woman, slept on it, then shared with my brothers, there could've been another outcome already. I should've ridden for Maliki the moment Savannah told me what was up so I could take care of him right then. Now my angel could possibly die, and so help me, if that happens, I'll never forgive myself.

I wrench open my back door and leap over the four foot or so wooden wall they have on all the apartments. It's our own private balcony area that most people decorate with chairs and shit. Mine's bare. My life's at the club or with Savannah. I don't spend time outside on my back porch. I wouldn't put it past some shit bags to steal people's stuff on the ground level that they leave out in the open. I don't trust easily. It has nothing to do with my background; it's just good common sense. People seem to be missing it more and more these days.

I take off in a sprint, worried out of my mind. It only takes me seconds to get to her back porch, but it feels like minutes. I reach for her balcony wall, using it to help propel me over the wood barrier. I land hard but shake it off, breathing deeply.

I inhale, collecting my wits. The pounding of my heart is so prominent that I struggle as I lay my head against the back door in an attempt to hear anything. I can't make out words, but I do hear a man's voice, reassuring me that Maliki's still here. He's talking to someone, but their tone is much lower. I'm going to guess it's Savannah, and she's still alive. *Thank God.* I can't wait to pump these motherfuckers full of lead for encroaching on my woman.

This explains why she never texted me back. Fuck! I hope he hasn't been here this entire time. If only I'd been more persistent and stayed behind to drive her to work…but then he could've killed me immediately, and she'd have no one to save her. It had to happen this way for a reason, so I could get to her before it's too late.

As carefully and quietly as possible, I insert my key into the top and then the lower lock. If they're in the kitchen, there's no possible way to miss me coming in through the back door. If they're in the living room, I'll have seconds before I'm discovered. Somehow, I doubt Maliki isn't the type to forgo a weapon, and my bet is, as soon as I open this door, bullets will be flying.

Sapphire Knight

Bash

Chapter 13

She wasn't looking for a knight, she was looking for a sword.

- atticus

Savannah

A whimper escapes me as Maliki backhands me again. He's a psycho pig just like his brother was before I killed him. I knew he'd catch up to me eventually, but I didn't think it would happen today. I knew as soon as I saw him enter the diner I was in trouble. I'd escaped out the back door, hopped into Sebastian's car and took off to hide out at the apartment.

I'd gotten here and barely made it inside when I realized that coming here was a mistake. I should've stopped at the MC instead of driving all the way home, but I thought Sebastian would be back. He told me that he had to talk to the guys about everything and that he'd be back right after. I was at work for a few hours, which was more than enough time for him to beat me here. Or so I thought.

I'd foolishly believed I escaped work without anyone noticing me, and I was too panicked that I didn't see what vehicle they were in. When the SUV was behind me, I thought nothing of it. I scrambled out of Bash's

Charger and into my apartment in a rush, too quickly to notice the large SUV slowing down and turning in behind me. I'd just closed the door and was twisting the lock on the handle when it was kicked in. The force was great enough, it propelled me backward. I'd gone sprawling to the floor, bracing as best I could to protect my stomach. Even with the bright sun blindingly surrounding his frame in the doorway, there was no mistaking Maliki. He reminded me of the reaper—dark and angry—coming to collect my death.

I may've been strong enough to kill his brother in cold blood, but I had time to plan it all out. I had a list that I checked each time I needed reminding of the next step to take. Being patient had paid off, and the opportunity finally presented itself. He'd foolishly believed he was untouchable, but I proved him wrong.

As I'd slid under his luxurious sheets, I'd rested my left hand on his chest. He thought it was because I was a horny slut for him. In reality, I was getting in a position to brace him. My right hand was safely tucked under the pillow with the insanely sharp scalpel. There're so many murder weapons you can choose, but I knew I needed something that would kill almost effortlessly. A murder weapon I could conceal easily but would work effectively. What better object than one that's often used to save lives.

My best friend works in a doctor's office, so getting what I needed was almost too easy. I lied and told her I needed a scalpel to cut off a wart. It was simple enough that with the right amount of persistence, she gave in and got me one. She said it was extra sharp because she didn't want me to be in pain trying to saw it off. Hell, she even offered to help me remove it. She had no idea she was aiding in getting a murder weapon, and she'll never know, for that matter. She doesn't deserve to have to live with any sort of guilt the knowledge may come with.

Once that scum dozed off, I made my move. I was silent and deadly, just like the serpent I'd intended to be. With my arm resting firmly on his chest, I'd reached up and stroked the side of his neck with my finger. I inhaled a deep breath, leaned up, and pulled my right hand free. I didn't give myself any time to think, I drove the blade straight into the side of his throat. It was so sharp, the blade slid in through his flesh like butter, slicing everything in its path. Blood gushed everywhere, spraying my face and neck as he gurgled, choking on the thick liquid.

You'd think I'd feel guilty about killing him, but I didn't. I still don't. He ruined my father and murdered him. There was no room in my heart or mind to sympathize with someone like that. Fuck him. God rest my father's soul. If he was watching from above, I pray he felt closure at that moment. My father may've been a victim, but I refused to allow his death to make me a casualty as well.

I sought retribution, and it was the best feeling in the world at the time. You ever hear that saying about a woman scorned? It's true. Men have to be careful of the women they choose to make enemies of. Some of us won't sit back and take it. Some of us fight back and kill if we have to.

My cheek stings as Maliki's slap resonates, bringing me back into the present. I wish I'd killed him, too, but there was no way he'd have allowed me to get that close. Maliki is smarter, I've come to learn, and it's probably why he's still alive.

"I warned Jerome that you were nothing but a sneaky slut. He should've listened to me. He was always too stubborn to take my word before thinking it over for a while. I know it was you! You killed him!"

My face is swollen already. I can feel it with the blood floating around in my mouth. He's kept me on my knees before him. Each time I've tried getting up or crawling away, he either strikes me or drags me by my hair to where he wants me. He hasn't punched me yet. I'm assuming he plans on drawing this out. While slaps may not seem like a big deal, it's a different story coming from a large man like Maliki. His hand is the size of my face, and his arms are solid with muscle. Just because he wears a tailored suit, doesn't mean he's not deadly.

"You seduced him and killed him when he was vulnerable. You know what I plan on doing to you? I'm going to beat you, rape you, and then kill you in your own bed, so you can know exactly how he felt in those last moments."

"I-I didn't beat or rape him," I argue stubbornly, shooting him a glower.

I'm all about self-preservation and saving my unborn child at all costs, but I won't hold back from speaking my truth. I admit I seduced him and killed him, but it was a kindness. I could've made his death much more miserable. I'd contemplated so many options, one of my favorites being that I sedate him enough to torture him then allow him to bleed out. I figured that was a bit too much for me, though, and I wouldn't be able to handle it, no matter how angry and hurt I was. I knew it had to be effective and not drawn out so I could go through with it. The seduction and scalpel seemed like the best plan as he wouldn't see it coming, and I was right.

"You don't get a say in my plans, just like Jerome didn't with yours." He spits in my face.

I swear slaps hurt, but there's nothing quite like being spat on. It's beyond degrading and disgusting. I gag, fighting back the urge to puke. If I give him any reason to believe I'm pregnant, I offer him one more thing to try and take from me. He can do whatever he can to break me, but I'll never stop protecting my child, no matter what the cost. It's what a mother does, and while I may've not met this little one yet, it doesn't matter one bit when it comes to that mother's instinct.

"Mike!" he shouts toward the front door. He must have a man out there waiting for him. Frankly, I was surprised he didn't have a handful of guys with him as he broke in. When I was with Jerome, Maliki always had an entourage surrounding him, making him feel more important than he really is. "Give me your knife!" he demands, and the urge to throw up rolls through me again. The thought of him with a knife absolutely terrifies me.

I move as quickly as possible, jumping up to take off toward my back door. I get maybe two steps before burning pain skates down my scalp into my neck. He's grabbed my hair at the back of my head. He yanks me into his body, and I swear I feel hair tearing from my scalp. It hurts so badly that tears prick at my eyes as my breath leaves me in shock. I'm wrenched into the same spot I was moments before. Each attempt wears down my strength a touch more. I'm running off pure adrenaline and the need for survival. I can only imagine how broken down I'll be by the time he decides to finally kill me.

A part of me is wishing with everything I have that Sebastian comes home to help me before it's too late. The other part is terrified that if he does, he'll be overpowered, and I'll have to watch my sweet guy be tortured and killed. I know he's strong and can defend himself, but there's no telling how much backup Maliki has outside waiting for him. If I have to choose between Sebastian possibly saving me or the chance he'll die, I choose my death. The world needs more men like my Bash out there. He's got a good heart and someone as genuine as he is-is hard to come by.

"Where do you think you're going?" Maliki barks mockingly. "I've only begun with you."

I hate it that I'm crying in front of him, but I can't help it. He hurt me physically, and I'm so angry. Those two feelings mixed together have the tears leaking, whether I want them to or not. "I'm not going to just roll over and allow you to do as you please. If you think I don't have self-preservation, then you're even more delusional."

"You're mouthy. No wonder why Jerome was amused with you. Here I thought it was your cunt, but maybe it was more your mouth. Tell me, can you suck cock like a vacuum?"

I glare. "I'll bite your penis off if you bring it anywhere near my mouth!" I scream in revolt. I may be tiny compared to him, but I'm fierce. I'll fight him every step of the way, no matter how beaten down I become.

He chuckles, sounding every bit the evil monster I know he is. "I'm going to have fun torturing that attitude out of you." His hand comes down to collide with the side of my head. A jolt of pain radiates through my skull, and I swear I see spots. The front door opens, allowing a brief shock of sunlight to filter in before it's slammed closed once more.

Maliki chuckles darkly again, the sound sending goosebumps over my flesh. "Looky here, slut, time for those clothes to come off so I can see what I'm playing with. You know, you should feel honored. It's not often I get my hands dirty; that's what the help's for. They get messy while I sit back and watch, but you're a different story. You killed my flesh and blood, my brother. Now I'll return the favor. I already got to that friend of yours. She was easy to find. I fucked her then watched my men put a few bullets in her. You know she cried and asked for you? She begged me to let you be free, and I agreed. But, I lied."

Sobs wrack my chest at him speaking of my best friend. I did everything I could to leave her in the dark about all of this, and to hear Maliki's gotten to her and killed her already hits me deep. I'd pulled away from her since I came up with the plan to murder Jerome, but she'll always hold a special place in my heart. Knowing she died because of my actions makes me sick. Her poor family.

"I ha-ate you," I state with a broken whisper. I've lost nearly everything at the hands of these men. I can only pray Maliki never finds out about Bash and what he means to me. I love him. At this moment, there's no use trying to deny my feelings for Sebastian. I truly love that man and am grateful for the compassion and affection he's shown me over the last few months.

"The feeling's mutual." He takes a threatening lunge for me. My hands fly up in defense, but he's overwhelming. He grabs my shirt in his ruthless grip, using his other hand that's palming the enormous blade to rip through the front of my work shirt. A scream escapes me as his hand clamps down on my breast, ripping at my bra's cup.

The back door flies open, the light shining in. It's not as bright as the front since it's on the opposite side of the building. My eyes fly in that direction, staring into my kitchen at the figure sailing through the door. My mouth drops, a gasp leaving me as Sebastian storms toward me. Surrounded by light, he's my version of an avenging angel, and in turn, the most beautiful man I've ever seen before. I need him so badly and to have him here, now, it brings a fresh onslaught of tears.

"Down, Angel!" he bellows, and my eyes fly back to Maliki, taking in his expression and movements. The knife's dropped to the floor, forgotten, as Maliki reaches into his shoulder holster for a gun. "Not so fast, Maliki!" Bash booms, pointing his own weapon at the man hovering over me as he stops a few feet away from us both. I crouch to the floor, trying to do what Sebastian instructs, but also not wanting to be that vulnerable to Maliki's feet either. "You finish pulling that out, and I empty rounds into your motherfuckin' chest, you feel me? I'm filling every motherfucker you brought here with lead too."

"Wait, Bash?" Maliki sounds quizzical, his brow creasing as he stares my boyfriend down. "You know this woman?"

Sebastian nods, keeping his gaze trained on the threat. "Yep, and I won't allow you to hurt her. Not ever again."

Maliki chuckles, his brows high on his forehead in amusement and surprise. "You realize this will impact our deals, and you'll be stepping into my personal business. Men don't live for very long when they meddle in my affairs."

"Right now, you're in mine. That woman belongs to me."

"Well..." Maliki rests his hands on his hips, obviously not registering the depth of Bash's words. I catch a bit of my blood on his right knuckles, and it makes me wince. I know the only reason why I'm not in as much pain as I should be is because of the adrenaline. My fight or flight response kicked in, and when I tried to run, he caught me, and the new burst of adrenaline has helped mask the pain. "I think we can work something out where we each make her pay for what she's done to the both of us. You can drop your gun, friend, and we'll come to a mutual agreement."

Sebastian keeps his weapon firmly trained on him, flicking his eyes to me for merely a second. His neck reddens once he gets a closer look at me, his nostrils flaring as anger consumes him. This is about to go to another level in about two minutes when Maliki realizes Sebastian isn't trying to claim me for a debt I owe him. My man is here to save me, not give me up to this psycho billionaire. With both of their attention resolutely pinned on one another, my hand slides over, scrambling to grab the knife. If I'm going to die today, I'm going down fighting.

"She's mine, Maliki," Sebastian states obstinately.

My eyes remain fixated above me, gauging Maliki. There's no way I'll allow him to get the jump on Bash and hurt my man. I'd do anything to protect Sebastian as time and again, he's proven to me he'll take care of me in his own way as well. This instance is my turn to step up to the plate.

"Bash," Maliki attempts to reason again. "We'll work this out. There's no need to throw away our business relationship over debts we can both settle here and now. In fact, this will only solidify us more in the future. This will make our trust in each other grow, once we've finished with her." Maliki is always thinking about his influence on other people, and without those crazy parties he hosts each week, he won't be able to maintain as much influence over certain individuals.

"You fucking idiot." Sebastian scowls, anger marring his handsome features. My man is furious, to the point if I were opposed, I'd be petrified. "She's my woman with my kid. I'll kill you before you fucking touch her again," he growls, done with this exchange. He's ready to collect his pound of flesh, or in Maliki's case, about two hundred twenty pounds of flesh.

Sebastian's proclamation has blindsided him, and it's the only chance I have. I leap off the ground, knife in hand. I lunge straight for Maliki's stomach, planting the blade as deeply as I can. I don't have a lot of strength, but this is do or die, so I use every ounce of life preserving force I can muster up to shove that knife in as powerfully as possible.

His large hands go for my neck, his digits latching on and squeezing so tightly that I can no longer breathe. My vision goes fuzzy as blackness quickly creeps in along with a burning sensation in my throat, like lava being poured down my esophagus. My fingers fight with his grip, but I'm nowhere near as strong as he is, and in mere moments, I feel like I'm on the edge of death. I may've stabbed him, but he's holding onto my throat for dear life, choking me to death.

Another dark image is suddenly above us, the figure blurry and grayish. I watch him put something against Maliki's head, then there're multiple loud blasts. I'm so out of it, it's only darkened images and black spots. I don't even sense the brain matter and blood spray hitting my flesh. I can feel nothing but choking and fire. The noise is muddled with my lack of breathing. The clamp around my neck loosens almost immediately, yet I feel as if everything is in slow motion.

My body falls to the ground in a heap, and I lie still, trying to clear the blackness tinting my vision. There's a burst of light flooding the room again as the front door's thrown open. I hear more deafening blasts, which I manage to piece together as being gunshots. Another figure falls to the ground off to the side of the bright light. There are more shots, and then nothing. I don't realize I'm sobbing and croaking Bash's name repeatedly until he's there, snuggling me into his lap.

"Shh, Sweet Pea. I got you, Savannah. You're safe, I promise you. I'm here, Angel. No one is left to hurt you. I promise, baby. Shh."

My face is soaked from my tears, my throat dry and throbbing from Maliki choking me so harshly. Sebastian leans in, kissing my forehead several times, and wiping away the wetness on my cheeks. He's breathing hard, his own eyes red-rimmed. I'm shaking, a complete mess, but once I meet his concerned gaze and take in their familiar blue, it's like I can finally drag in a deep breath. "I love you," I manage to wheeze with a cough, my tone nearly silent.

"Fuck, babe. I love you, Savannah. *So. Fucking. Much.*" He peppers each word with a kiss on my forehead. His eyes fill with water as he looks me over. "Jesus, baby." He breathes the words brokenly. "He fucked you up. Goddamn it, I was too fucking late. Christ, I let him hurt you." The tears spill over, trailing down his pale face, and my heart aches to witness his sadness.

I try to swallow, the ache in my esophagus still burning with pain and whisper, "You were just in time. Thank you, *hero*."

"I'm no hero, Angel. If I were, I'd have been here when they showed up. None of this would've happened to you or to our baby."

I shake my head, everything throbbing with the move. "My hero, since the first day," I quietly argue.

His lip trembles before he leans in and kisses me again. He's not kissing anywhere but my forehead. My face must look as bad as it feels.

"Holy fuck, Bash! Any more here?" I hear, and then several shadows surround us. My vision has cleared enough for me to make everyone's faces out, thankfully, or it may've freaked me out seeing more large men come at us. It's Chaos. I take in his expression, along with the others' concerned features as they peer at us and have a quick look around at the dead bodies.

"I killed them all," Sebastian growls, holding me possessively. It feels good to be in his arms. There's no other place I'd rather be. Except, maybe our bed. I could really use a comfortable place to lie down while I deal with all of this discomfort.

Chaos barks, "North, Sly! Grab those bodies in the doorway and get them in here. We'll wait for a beat to see if the cops were called. If not, and the neighbors were smart enough to keep their fuckin' mouths closed, then we'll need to dispose of these bodies. Fuck! I can't believe this happened here and in the middle of the day. Christ."

Bash grumbles, "Need the doc. My woman's hurt and pregnant. If my baby's not okay, I'm gonna kill these motherfuckers all over again."

Jinx nods, attempting to calm my sweet man. "We know, brother. I called him as I was jogging to my bike. He should be here any minute to look your woman over. We have you, brother. You need anything, you say the word, and I got you."

Sebastian swallows, his Adam's apple bobbing as he remains staring at me. He peers at me as if I'm the most valuable thing he's ever seen before. "Never letting you go, Angel. Never gonna let anyone hurt you, not ever again. Don't give a fuck what I gotta do, it won't happen again, I swear it."

I nod, trying not to move my head much, as it sends shocks of pain everywhere. "I believe you," I whisper. I flash my gaze to Chaos and murmur as loudly as I can muster, "Bash's my hero. Love my hero."

Chaos nods, his regard serious. "I know, girl. Pretty sure you're his, too. You just don't realize it. Both of you are gonna be all right. I'll see to it."

Chapter 14

I wish you to know that you have been the last dream of my soul.

- Charles Dickens

Savannah's hospital room the following day

"Sir, visiting hours are over. I'm sorry, but you'll have to return tomorrow," the nurse informs me again in her annoying snippy tone.

I release a low, menacing growl, ready to pounce on her ass for trying to make me leave. I flick my concerned stare back to Savannah. "This is why I didn't want you at the goddamn hospital," I huff to my angel, ignoring the nurse. "I can have the doc at the club monitor you instead, just say the word. I'll take care of you. You're my woman. *Mine.*" And I mean every word of it, too. These people here are driving me fucking crazy. They won't tell me shit with what's going on. I keep stealing her chart to stay updated on everything.

"Sir!" the nurse chirps, further maddening my thoughts, flaring my temper. If she had any idea of what my ol' lady and I just went through together, she'd keep her space and her thoughts to herself.

I spin on her, getting in her face. "Look, lady, if you think I'm leaving my woman after she was attacked, you've got another thing coming!" I rumble, making her jump. "I highly suggest you don't ask me to fucking leave her again, cause it ain't happening! I won't *ever* leave her." I've been hovering a bit over Savannah, but what can anyone expect. I don't know if anybody associated with Maliki will be coming after her yet, and I'll be damned if they get anywhere near her. I won't be able to breathe easy on it until my club finds out more intel on the piece of shit.

Chaos chuckles, attempting to ease a bit of the tension radiating through the small hospital room. "Ma'am, let's have a chat." He interrupts my tirade before I end up with security called on me for tossing the nurse out of my woman's room.

I know she's only doing her job, and I commend her for it, but I'm doing mine as well. It's up to me to protect Savannah, and I haven't done a good enough job in the past. That changes now. I plan to be within three feet of her the entire stay at this hospital unless one of us is pissing. In that case, I'll wait on the other side of the door while she handles her business. The staff around here better get used to it and quickly. I didn't leave last night, and I won't go today either.

I hear Chaos's deep tone out in the hallway reverberate through the door. "Savannah Lexington is his ol' lady. That's his *wife* in our world. They've been through some serious shit recently if you can't tell by her face and his overbearingness. Now, I can have my prospect order you folks some dinner or something, courtesy of the club. Try to help make up for his attitude, but I know my brother, and Bash won't be leaving that room without his woman. I'm also aware you don't want Savannah checking out just yet, so this is the only way."

I'm surprised he's aiming to rationalize with her, but I'm grateful for it. We're used to demanding shit so often, that we often forget that sometimes a situation can use a bit of finesse to get what we need. You ever hear that saying you can attract more bees with honey? Well, Chaos's working his charm, and the ladies don't ever seem to hesitate to fall for it either.

I forget about what's going on out in the hallway, sending a tender look at my angel. She's lying here appearing just as helpless as last night, even though I know she's anything but. The doctor and nurses haven't let her do much of anything since we arrived. They want to monitor her, and I know it's driving my stubborn woman a bit crazy. "How you doin', babe?" I haven't left her side, and I've asked her the same question pretty much every hour. I'm determined to make sure she has whatever she needs.

Savannah sighs, setting the remote down. One of her eyes is swollen shut, and she's been struggling to watch anything with her open eye. She says it gives her a headache, and knowing she is in any kind of discomfort makes me want to bring that fucker Maliki back to life so I can torture him. She doesn't deserve any of this. Savannah's been through enough to last a lifetime already. "I wish we could go home."

I grunt, agreeing with her, but not admitting to it out loud. While it'd be great to have privacy, I like knowing she has a team of people looking after her and our baby, in case either one of them needs anything. "Tomorrow, Sweet Pea," I promise, glancing up to the monitors. Savannah's had on this elastic belt thing around her small tummy since we showed up, and it's been keeping up with our baby's heartbeat. I like seeing hers and the baby's hearts beating on the screen before me. It gives me a small sense of comfort with the proof they're still here and alive.

"Come lay with me," she requests. Comfort washes over me at her invitation, and I do as she asks. I'll do anything to make her happy now and in the future. We take life for granted too much. Yesterday's incident was my come-to-Jesus moment. I won't waste time or take my woman for granted ever. Life is far too fucking precious. People need to wake up and realize it before it's too late.

Moving slowly and carefully, I crawl into the single size hospital bed. I remain on my side, facing her, attempting to take up as little bit of the space as possible. I slept in this same spot last night, much to the hospital's dismay. There was no way in hell that they were peeling me away from holding her, no matter how vigilant I had to be not to bump her or whatever. I was overly concerned she'd end up with nightmares, and I wanted to be close so I could console her if she needed me.

"You sure this isn't hurting you?" I check with her, the same as I did last night and this morning. I've been as gentle with her as I can manage.

Savannah's face is bruised up with a horrifying array of colors, ranging from purplish black to blue. It has me automatically thinking her body is just as bruised up, and I wish I could take her place. Thankfully, the rest of her isn't as beat up. I've seen it with my own eyes when she initially got checked out. I know her creamy flesh is unharmed, aside from bruising on her upper arms and neck, anyhow. Yet, I still fight with the gut-wrenching feeling each time that I glance at her face. My beautiful woman looks nothing like she usually does, and it makes me rabid inside with rage and heartache. I've been trying to hide it, but I know my brothers can see right through my charade of calm. I've kept up the façade for her. She doesn't need to witness me any more distraught than she already has.

"I want you close. Please hold me." She's been whispering brokenly too.

The doctor didn't want her attempting to speak at all yesterday. She was so emotionally shaken up, they gave her a mild sedative in the end so they could run as many tests as they needed without disturbing her further. Today she's been whispering here and there. I asked about her throat when she woke up, and she told us that it still hurts badly. I've been giving her ice chips, but I know they can't take the pain away completely, and it cuts at me that I can't do more to make her comfortable. The doctor says she's lucky her vocal cords weren't damaged when Maliki nearly crushed her throat.

"Anything for you, Angel. Whatever you need, you let me know, and I'll make it happen."

She tilts her head to lightly rest her temple against my forehead. My hand instantly seeks out her stomach, protectively resting over the baby. Ever since I saw the ultrasound they did on her yesterday, I can't stop touching her belly. The baby is tiny, we couldn't tell the sex yet, but that didn't matter. The most important thing was everything inside looked like it should, according to the hospital staff. The tot was moving, and there was a strong, quick heartbeat. The tech was cool enough to print us out a few snapshots of our tiny baby bean, and amongst all the terror yesterday, we had a little piece of joy to focus on.

"I love you, Sebastian," she murmurs, a bit dazed from the last dose of pain killers the doc gave her. He reassured us both the meds wouldn't hurt the child, and she wouldn't get much more, so we needn't worry. I've learned that where Savannah and our child is concerned, I will never stop worrying.

"I love you, too. I'm so fucking grateful you two are okay. I'll never forgive myself for not figuring it out and getting to you sooner."

She mumbles, "You had no way of knowing. You were already at your club talking to your brothers about how to protect me. Besides, you showed up right when I needed you the most."

"Judging by him hitting you so many times, you needed me much earlier." The words choke me as I admit my failure.

"No, you don't understand." I gaze at her curiously as tears swim in her one eye that she has open. "H-he was cutting through my clothes when you stormed in."

"Bastard," I swear. That explains why her shirt was torn apart. I haven't asked much about yesterday, and the doctor has kept the cops away for the most part so far. Still, I know she hasn't let me in on all the details that went down between her and Maliki yesterday.

"He was going to r-r-rape me and kill me. You don't know how perfect your timing was."

"Christ, Angel." I breathe. My insides feel like they're being shredded at that thought. "Goddamn. I wish I could bring him back and torture him for weeks for what he's done to you. The thought of him threatening to do those things to you, I-I don't know how to handle that right now without combusting and completely losing my shit."

She brings her hand to my cheek. "Sebastian, you're where I need you right now. You're here, next to me, being my anchor. I would be lost if I didn't have you with me, *truly lost*. You can't keep thinking of what you should've done." Her voice breaks, and she has to stop and swallow a few times before she can quietly continue. "You killed him for me. You saved both of us. I will always love you for what you've sacrificed for us."

"There was no sacrifice, baby, I will do whatever's necessary to protect you and help you in any way possible. You and our baby. I love you too fucking much to let you go through life without me having your back, precious woman."

I want to wipe away her tears, but I'm too damn frightened I'll hurt her even more. I shouldn't have to worry about my touch harming my woman, but today I do. It's a lesson I'll never forget either. Savannah may be strong enough to take care of her problems on her own terms, but one thing is certain, she'll never have to do it alone again. It's a silent vow I make to myself and her, as I watch my beautiful woman eventually find sleep. I'm here in case she needs anything, and I won't ever go anywhere, for as long as she'll have me.

Church

Two weeks after Savannah's home from the hospital...

"How's your woman?" the brothers ask. It's been two weeks since she's been back home. I moved her shit to my apartment for the time being. I could tell going back to her place was freaking her out a little too much. It's only temporary, as I've been checking out the paper for any decent local listings. Savannah and my kid deserve more than to be cramped in a tiny one-bedroom apartment.

"Not happy. She still can't work. The bruising is getting better, but you can still see it through her makeup. The boss said he doesn't want her in until it's completely gone, so she doesn't give customers anything to talk about. I guess he's determined this had to be a club situation she got dragged into, and he doesn't want to be affiliated in any way with it. Stupid motherfucker. I wanted to beat his ass, but Sav made me promise to leave him alone."

Sly scowls. "That's some shit."

I nod. "She's acting like everything's okay, but I hear her dreaming at night. It's the whole reason I got her to move out of her apartment and into mine in the first place. She's a strong woman, but nightmares haunt everyone. Unfortunately, that includes her."

"She been talking it over with you?" Jinx asks.

I shrug. "Yes and no. I can see her processing shit on and off. She hasn't wanted to come to the compound, but I'm going to surprise her and bring her. She needs to be around people, some who actually give a fuck."

Chaos grunts. "No one will mess with her here. She'll always be safe with us."

I know, that's why I want her here. I trust my brothers with my life, and in that sense, my woman's. "Appreciate that. Thank fuck there wasn't anything wrong with the baby too. I've never been so worried in my life, and I haven't even met the kid yet."

Jinx flashes a grin. "It's only just beginning, brother."

I meet North's somber gaze. "You find out anything else on Maliki?"

The brothers perk up at my question, their gaze beating down on North for answers. Being the enforcer, I know I can count on him to take care of any loose ends. We didn't get much of a chance to prepare for anything since Maliki struck while we were discussing him. "I went by the addresses you gave me, did a little recon. I got rid of a few people at his warehouse, but otherwise, there hasn't been much else going on. His company is organizing his funeral and shit, but I haven't found anyone in particular poking around. He had an assistant who's been arranging the service and having Maliki's house packed up. The only family I can find is his dead brother and a long-lost cousin. We'll have to sit and wait a bit, but I don't anticipate any retaliation. That father you mentioned a while back didn't check out. He died some time ago as well. Looking closer, I wouldn't be surprised if it was the two prick brothers that offed him."

I release a tense breath. "Good to know. Hopefully, my woman can finally relax and stop hiding away from now on."

Chaos murmurs, "She deserves to live her life. Can't believe she's been dealin' with all this like she has. Your ol' lady is a keeper, brother."

"Thanks, Prez." I agree. I wouldn't give her up for the world. She's proven herself time and again that she's exactly the type of strong, but sweet woman I need in my life to help balance me out.

He continues, "Other than keeping an eye on Maliki's associates, we don't have much going on this week. Anyone have something to be discussed in church?"

"Centerfolds," North growls, garnering all of our attention. "I'm going to be over there more this week. I may need a few of you around. Some asshole and his buddies keep stopping in and stirring up trouble."

Jinx brows shoot up. "They have a lot of fucking nerve."

Chaos huffs. "We can't have shit going on at the strip club. We don't need that headache, being one of the few spots around here that can serve liquor. We don't want to fuck up any of our chances with our grandfather clause. You know as well as I do, if something goes down and we lose our liquor license, we'll never get it back for that location."

North grunts his agreement. "Exactly why I'm nipping that shit in the bud, ASAP."

"Anyone got an issue with helping out?" Chaos flicks his gaze to each of his officers. None of us speak up. "Anything else we need to discuss?" Again, we're quiet. "All right, then, church dismissed!" He slams the gavel down, and as the noise reverberates through the space, I quickly stand.

"I'm out, brothers, gotta get back to my woman." I say my goodbyes and head for the apartment as quickly as possible. Any moment away from Savannah is a moment too long.

Sapphire Knight

Bash

Chapter 15

Just because I love you, it doesn't mean I won't kill you. It just means
I'll bury you in a nice place with flowers and shit.

- tattoosplendour.com

Savannah

Seven weeks later...

"Can't wait until you can be on the back of my bike again. I miss your fine ass snuggled up to my back, Angel," Bash rasps as he pulls his Charger into the MC parking lot. It's a full house with all of his brothers' bikes parked out front along with a few vehicles I don't recognize.

"Not sure how often that'll happen with an infant to tote around."

He grins and with a shrug, says good-naturedly, "You're right, Sweet Pea. I should probably trade this in for a bigger cage. You'll need it hauling our bunch around."

My heart rate beats wildly in my chest at his words, and I sputter. "B-bunch? Excuse me? We're having one."

His smile grows. "Yeah, for now. You really think I can keep my hands—or my dick, for that matter—away from you? You remember what happened the last time my dick got near you, right?"

I point at my stomach and smirk. "Well, no shit, Sherlock."

He chuckles, shaking his head as he throws the car in park and hops out. Rounding in front of the Charger, he comes to my side and opens my door. He does it all the time, always right by my side to make me feel safe. I love him even more for it too. "How about we strike a deal."

"Oh, heavens, why am I getting anxiety with this?"

He snickers some more. I love it that my man is always smiling and laughing around me. It makes me feel like I'm doing something right. "Probably cause you're one intelligent bitch who knows her ol' man."

I lean in, offering a kiss at his compliment. It took some warming up to grow accustomed to their MC terms, but now I know he's not being ugly. Just like him claiming me or being his property is another compliment, it's him taking responsibility for me and pledging to care for me always. A man willing to commit that strongly to a woman says something about their character. In Bash's case, his is golden, and I'm one lucky woman to have a man who cherishes me so much. "Out with it, VP."

"You can pick out any SUV you want if you give me another kid."

My footsteps falter, and I pause outside in the heat. He stops next to me, his playful gaze meeting mine. My smile drops as I hold his hand a bit tighter. "You weren't joking?"

He grows serious and shakes his head. "No, Angel. I want a family with you. I love you."

I bite my lip, not needing any more time or reassurance to think it over. I nod, pushing up on my tiptoes to kiss his lips. His arms wrap around my waist as his forehead gently leans against mine and allows me to peck his lips a few times. I state quietly, "I love you, too, Sebastian. Let's have this sweet little pea, then we'll work on having another once I'm healed. I want a family with you too." And if we have another that ends up being a girl, maybe I can name her after my best friend whose life was taken because of me. She deserves to be honored for her spirit to live on.

I start to tear up, my feet going flat again, and I laugh. "Damn hormones." I wave them off, stepping back from his hold, but keeping my fingers linked with his. Ever since everything went down, my man is always touching me in one way or another and double-checking everything to make sure I'm safe and happy. I know he'll make an absolutely amazing father when the time comes for us to meet our child.

"You make me the happiest man, Savannah. Never in my life would've thought a wreck was my blessing in disguise."

"I couldn't agree more," I say, using my free hand to smooth down my sundress. My closet has grown immensely since Bash has come into my life. The man is forever having me order new sundresses. He practically wants me to live in them. I get benefits from it as well. He's still eating me out all the time in random places. The man is insatiable. "I can't wait to tell everyone what we're having! Is this why everybody is here? Did you tell them we found out?"

"Told 'em we'd be stopping by and to be around."

"Okay, good." I nod as he opens the door and waits for me to step inside ahead of him. I stride over the threshold, tugging him along with me, expecting to be greeted with the usual low volume rock music and bikers drinking beers at their bar.

"Surprise!" is shouted by multiple people, and I jump.

Sebastian's front comes to my back, and his arms wrap around my middle, his palms protectively resting over my small bump. He leans in until his lips are next to my ear as his deep voice lowly rasps, "Surprise, Momma."

I take everything in, tears making my gaze watery as my chest warms. There are balloons everywhere, along with a few signs and random pastel decorations. A table's set up with food and a cake, half of the table has a blue tablecloth and treats while the opposite is all pink. Everyone stands around smiling at us and talking amongst each other, their moods putting me at ease and happiness blooms inside me.

"They did this?"

"You deserve something special, baby. You deserve a baby shower, a chance to celebrate, and be happy."

Sebastian's mom and dad approach as I'm about to spin around and make out with my man, maybe drag him to his old room and fuck his brains out for being so good to me all the time. "There's my daughter!" Sebastian's mom exclaims, beaming brightly. With her here, I know she must be responsible for all the decorations, and it makes me adore her a little more for going to the trouble for us. I first met her when I was in the hospital after Maliki found me. Sebastian's mom is one of the kindest, most accepting women I've ever met. "Come here, doll," she calls and pulls me in, wrapping me in her warm mom embrace.

God, I missed this.

She says, "I'm so happy we get to find out what my grandchild is going to be today," she exclaims, rocking me back and forth until Sebastian releases me with a chuckle so his mom can continue to be excited with me. She pulls back, still holding my arms. "Now everything we got is in neutral colors, but if you want, we can exchange them for anything specific. This is your day, honey, and Sebby wants it perfect, as do I."

I nearly choke, wanting to tell them that it's already the best, just having them here supporting us. The day was going to be great, regardless, knowing we were planning to tell Sebastian's brothers what we're having, but to see that everyone did this…it's so much. These people really have become my family over the short amount of time I've been around. They've welcomed me in with open arms, gave me their protection, their friendship and one of their members to keep forever.

Sebastian's dad leans in with a hug next. "Savannah, you look radiant. You make such a pretty momma." Tears track down my cheeks, and I quickly move to swipe them away. I'm so overcome with emotion. I'm pregnant and full of hormones, but to have a family again after it was so ruthlessly stolen from me, I can't help but cry from happiness, hope, and love.

Chaos's ol' lady flashes me a bright smile. I don't know her well, except that she's nice and been through her own share of issues. I'm hoping that we'll grow closer over time. I haven't been around her much with everything going on and working. Sebastian wants to include me in the club more, he's mentioned it, so hopefully, Chaos's ol' lady will end up becoming a longtime friend. It would be weird if we didn't like each other since our guys are so close.

"I'm so happy," I manage to acknowledge, and Sebastian flashes a wide, joyful smile at me.

"That's all I want, Angel. Now, would you like to tell everyone about our baby, or me?" After seeing what he helped plan for me, I nod my head at him. He can have this moment of excitement. I've already gotten everything I could want. He beams, yanking me to him to tuck me under his arm. He shouts enthusiastically, "We're having a baby, Bash! Get ready, *motherfuckers,* there's about to be a mini me around here!"

His brothers hoot and holler, making me laugh as they head over to congratulate us and slap him on the back. Sebastian's parents come over to hug me again and tell me how excited they are for us. I promise we'll visit a lot and they say the same. Family is everything, and I'm glad they feel that way as well. I already know we'll have the MC around forever. It's my man's second family and now mine as well.

A few people from work offer me quick hugs and tell me they'll fill in for me if I ever need a day off. They have kids and say that they know how it is. I don't know what they mean just yet, but I appreciate their offers. It's nice to have a few people from the diner show up for this too and be allowed to see a different side of the MC.

Chaos steps in front of me, along with his woman. She offers me a friendly smile while he stares down at me wearing a serious expression. "Prez," I greet, showing him the respect he deserves for running this club. The guys have chastised me on several occasions that I don't need to address them as so, but I kind of like it. It makes me feel like I fit in with them, and everyone wants some sort of acceptance in their lives. I have it with Sebastian, so, naturally, I want it here, too. He loves these guys in his own way.

Chaos breaks out into a grin. He doesn't share them often, so I know it's reserved for special moments. "Happy for you, girl. Proud to call you an ol' lady of this club."

I flash him a soft smile. He's like the older, gruff brother I never had before and never realized I needed until coming here. "Thank you, Chaos. I'm proud to call you my family," I return, and I think it catches him off guard.

He tilts his head, and then almost as if he silently says fuck it, he leans in and offers me a hug. These guys aren't big huggers, especially to another brother's woman, so I take it as the gift it is. He's welcomed me into his club and has given me his blessing to be with his brother and best friend. That's a pretty damn good feeling. His ol' lady leans in to embrace me once Chaos has moved out of the way, whispering, "I'm excited for you and Bash."

"Thank you," I reply, and the other guys congratulate me as well. The moment fades into the background, but it's a memory I won't ever forget.

Bash presses a kiss to my temple. "You're not crushing on my prez, hm? Gonna make me jealous?" I can feel his grin against my skin, and I shake my head.

I meet his gaze, wearing a tender smile. "Never, that man is my brother now too. He was congratulating us, and it was a big compliment coming from your best friend, babe. I don't ever want to cause problems for your club or your brothers. This is your life, and I'm a part of that now too."

His hand goes to my chin, and he tilts my face up, his cobalt irises taking me in. He shakes his head. "You're wrong."

I swallow tightly, suddenly not feeling so confident with everything. "I am?"

"This isn't my life, it used to be. This is my club, my brothers. You and our baby are *my life*."

"I love you."

"I love you too, Angel. *Forever*."

"*Forever*."

Sapphire Knight

Epilogue

Forever is composed of nows.

- Emily Dickinson

Savannah's water just broke, and now she's freaking out...

"I can't believe all of this hasn't made you want to run away from me," she murmurs, looking a little lost and broken. Her pregnancy is making her worry overtime. Now that the baby's coming, she's afraid I'm not going to stick around, but she couldn't be further from the truth. A little labor and delivery won't scare me off, especially not when I plan on knocking her up again as soon as she'll allow me to.

"Angel, I'm a thirty-two-year-old man. I've lived long enough that these issues we've gone through don't mean anything to me. Aside from me making sure everything is taken care of, however that may be. I'm old enough to be ready for a family; you and the pregnancy have been the light in my life so far. The shit storm you were dealing with, never should've been at your door in the first place. You fell victim to a duo of predators, and you never deserved to go through any of it. I'll always protect you from any problems I can. Running away from you is the very last thing I want; in fact, I think it's time we made it official."

"What?"

"That you're my ol' lady, my woman. We've mentioned it in passing, but it's overdue that we have a serious discussion on it. There won't ever be another for me, Savannah. You're it for me. Also that we're living together. I'm getting rid of my apartment, and we're gonna find a nice house with a yard and a garage that you love. We'll buy it, and we'll raise our family there."

Her brow wrinkles as her mind races with my words. "You would do all of this for me and our baby, Bash?"

"I'd do so much more, Savannah. All you have to do is ask, baby. I meant it when I told you that you're my whole world."

She bites her bottom lip, her eyes falling to the ground before determination steals over her regard, and she meets my curious stare. "Would you marry me?"

I swallow, not expecting that. She always has a way of throwing me off-kilter. "Is that what you want?" *It may be hard while she's pushing out my kid, but where there's a will, there's a way, and I'll somehow figure out a way to make it happen.*

"If my father were still alive, he'd insist on it. In our culture, you're married before having a child…well, that's how it's preached anyhow."

"We don't have to follow anything we don't want to." Besides, her water already broke. I'd say it's a little too late for us to be following all the traditions now.

She nods, releasing a breath. "I know, but it would've made him proud of me."

"I'd bet a million times over that he's prouder of you than you can ever imagine."

Tears fill her eyes. "I hope so, but I want to honor him this way."

"I would love to marry you, don't get me wrong, but I will only do it if it's what you want, not for your old man. Tell me, baby, you wanna marry me because you love me and can't imagine your future without me being in it?" I ask, ready to fall down on bended knee if she were to agree. I don't plan on ever letting her go, regardless of if we're married or not. I've already committed myself to her and our son. That won't change in the slightest whether she has a ring on her finger or not. She'll have my property patch on her, and that's proof enough for me.

Her lip trembles, and with it, fresh tears fall. She whispers, "I do love you, Sebastian. I want to marry you more than anything."

With a swift nod, I bend, holding her hand in mine. "I love you, Angel. I promise to cherish and protect you always. I promise to hold you and our children near to my heart, and always put my family above all else. I promise to be your ol' man, if you'll be my ol' lady…will you do me the honor of becoming my wife and my partner?

"Oh, honey," she breathes. "Yes, yes, yes!"

I leap up, wrapping her in my arms, wearing a smile so wide it makes my face hurt. "You're mine," I growl, leaning my forehead against hers, wanting a kiss.

I'll be texting my brothers in about two minutes to discuss this marriage. I don't care if they have to kidnap a priest for me, I need one ASAP. First of all, however, I need to drive my woman to the hospital. Her safety and well-being are above all else, no matter how much I wish I could shower her with love for the rest of the day. We're having a kid today, and my world is becoming even more complete.

"I am yours." She flashes me a grin as I help her to the car. "And you're mine too."

"Forever, Angel." I lean in, taking her mouth with mine, sealing our fate with a promise and a kiss.

Sapphire Knight

Bash Thank You

Thank you so much for reading Bash! I hope you enjoyed Sebastian and Savannah. I love writing about my alpha asshole heroes, but sometimes we don't need a man to come in and save us. Sometimes, we want to have someone in our corner cheering us on and that's enough. I'm fortunate enough to have fifteen years with my OTTA. He's saved me, let me save him, and also stands in my corner cheering me on when I'm being my own hero. For everyone who doesn't have that special somebody, now *you have Bash*.

XO- Sapphire Knight #BeYourOwnHero

Sapphire Knight

Bash

Acknowledgements

My husband – This life wouldn't be possible without having your continued support. I know it's not always easy when I zone out on my laptop and don't want to be disturbed. I appreciate you rolling with it and embracing my chosen career. I'm glad you've discovered a way to implement Knight Creations business to fit so well with mine. I wouldn't want to spend my life with anyone else. I love you, I'm thankful for you, I can't say it enough.

My boys – You're my whole world. I love you both. This never changes, and you better not be reading these books until you're thirty and tell yourself your momma did not write them! I can never express how grateful I am for your support. You are quick to tell me that my career makes you proud, that I make you proud. As far as mom wins go, that one takes the cake. I love you with every beat of my heart, and I will forever.

My Beta Babes – This wouldn't be possible without you always being there to cheer me on. I can't express my gratitude enough for each of you. I'm blessed to have your continued support.

Editor Mitzi Carroll –Mitzi, I couldn't do this without you. You always polish my work up while not attempting to smother my voice and I greatly appreciate it. You are the best! Thank you for pouring tons of hours into my passion and being so wonderful to me. Thank you for your amazing support and always being there whenever I need you.

Marisa Nichols Proofreading/Alated Bibliophile thank you for proofreading Bastard, I enjoy reading your comments with Mitzi's. You two make my day! It's an honor to have you two in my corner.

CT Cover Creations – A huge thank you for your help on this unique project! I can always count on you and that means so much. Thank you for all of your hard work and the kindness you don't ever hesitate to share with me. Your designs are superb and your professionalism is on

Sapphire Knight

another level entirely. You set the bar high with designers and you've completely spoiled me. Thank you!

A special thank you to M.N. Forgy for dreaming up this project and inviting me to be a part of it. To my fellow Authors in the Kings of Carnage project, I admire you a great deal and am honored to have made this little world come together with you.

Hilary Storm, thank you for being so goddamn awesome. I love you and am grateful to call you my friend. You are a force and I admire your commitment, your talent, and your genuineness. You are the realist person I know and consider you my friend for life.

My Blogger Friends – YOU ARE AMAZING! No, really, you are. You take a new chance on me with each book and in return, share my passion with the world. You never truly get enough credit, and I'm forever grateful! There are so many of you that have stuck with me from the beginning, that dedication is truly humbling.

My Readers – I love you. You make my life possible, thank you. I can't wait to meet many of you this year and in the future. To those of you leaving me the awesome spoiler free reviews, you motivate me to keep writing. For that, I will forever be grateful, as this is my passion in life.

And as always, ADOPT DON'T SHOP! Save a life today and adopt from a rescue or your local animal shelter. #ProudDobermanMom

Bash

Also By Sapphire

Oath Keepers MC Series
Secrets
Exposed
Relinquish
Forsaken Control
Friction
Princess
Sweet Surrender – free short story
Love and Obey – free short story
Daydream
Baby
Chevelle
Cherry
Heathen

Russkaya Mafiya Series
Secrets
Corrupted
Corrupted Counterparts – free short story
Unwanted Sacrifices
Undercover Intentions

Dirty Down South Series
Freight Train
3 Times the Heat
2 Times the Bliss

Complete Standalones
Gangster
Unexpected Forfeit
The Main Event – free short story
Oath Keepers MC Collection
Russian Roulette

Sapphire Knight
Tease – Short Story Collection
Oath Keepers MC Hybrid Collection
Vendetti
Viking - free newsletter short story

Capo Dei Capi Vendetti Duet
The Vendetti Empire - part 1
The Vendetti Queen - part 2
The Vendetti Seven (Coming Soon)

Harvard Academy Elite Duet
Little White Lies
Ugly Dark Truth

Royal Bastards MC TEXAS
Bastard

Kings of Carnage MC Series
Bash – Vice President

Bash

Keep In Touch

Website

www.authorsapphireknight.com

Newsletter

bit.ly/SKnightNewsletter

Facebook

www.facebook.com/AuthorSapphireKnight

BookBub

www.bookbub.com/profile/sapphire-knight

Made in the USA
Middletown, DE
19 January 2025

69812973R00106